THIS BEAUTIFUL LIFE

THIS
BEAUTIFUL
LIFE

A Novel

HELEN SCHULMAN

HARPER

An Imprint of HarperCollinsPublishers
www.harpercollins.com

THIS BEAUTIFUL LIFE. Copyright © 2011 by Helen Schulman. All rights reserved. Printed in the United States of America. No part of this book may be used or reproduced in any manner whatsoever without written permission except in the case of brief quotations embodied in critical articles and reviews. For information, address HarperCollins Publishers, 10 East 53rd Street, New York, NY 10022.

HarperCollins books may be purchased for educational, business, or sales promotional use. For information, please write: Special Markets Department, HarperCollins Publishers, 10 East 53rd Street, New York, NY 10022.

FIRST EDITION

Designed by Jennifer Ann Daddio / Bookmark Design & Media Inc.

Library of Congress Cataloging-in-Publication Data has been applied for.

ISBN: 978-0-06-202438-1

11   12   13   14   15   OV/RRD   10   9   8   7   6   5   4

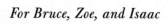

For Bruce, Zoe, and Isaac

Lord, give us what you have already given.

—*Ilya Kaminsky, "Envoi"*

THIS BEAUTIFUL LIFE

. . .

H ER MOUTH FILLED THE screen. Purple lip gloss, clear braces.

"Still think I'm too young?"

She leaned over, the fixed lens of the camera catching a tiny smattering of blemishes on her cheek, like a comet's spray. Her hair had been bleached white, with long blond roots, and most of it was pulled back and up into a chunky ponytail above the three plastic hoops climbing the rim of her ear.

The song began to play, Beyoncé. *I love to love you, baby.* She stepped aside, revealing her room in all its messy glory. Above the bed was a painting; the central image was a daisy. A large lava lamp bubbled and gooed on the nightstand.

She was giggling offstage. Suddenly, the screen was a swirl of green plaid. Filmstrips of color in knife pleats. Her short skirt swayed along with her round hips. A little roll of ivory fat nestled above the waistband. She wore a white tank top, which she took off, her hands quickly finding the cups of her black bra. The breasts inside were small, and at first she covered them with her palms, fingers splayed like scallop shells. Then she unhooked the bra in the front and they popped out as if on springs. Her hands did a little fan dance as they reached below her hemline and lifted up her skirt.

She'd done all of this for his benefit. To please him. To prove him wrong. She reached out for the little toy baseball bat and the next part was hard to watch, even if you knew what was coming.

Except it wasn't.

• • •

———————

As with so many things of consequence, it all began with a party.

Two parties. Both of Elizabeth Bergamot's children had parties to go to. Jake, the eldest—his longish brown hair suddenly grazing his collarbones, his eyes the color of muddled mint—was on his own that night, of course. His party was up in the Bronx, in Riverdale, somewhere near his school. He was fifteen and a half the previous Friday. It was pretty ridiculous that the Bergamots continued to celebrate this increasingly minor milestone—his half birthday—with half a cake and half a present. Richard, Liz's husband, had started the whole business ten years earlier, when he'd surprised them both by bringing home half a deck of cards that year, the other twenty-six miraculously appearing overnight under the boy's pillow.

"He's five and a half on Cinco de Mayo," Richard had said, by way of explanation. "Is there a better cause for celebration?"

Since the gesture was so touching, so sweet and fatherly, and Richard was a Californian by birth, Liz had trusted him on the import of such things, Mexican things. Plus, it seemed fun—a fun family tradition! It was what Liz had always hungered after despite generations of contrary evidence: relatives as respite, home as haven, a retreat from the rest of the dangerous, damaging world.

Last Friday, *this* Cinco de Mayo, Jake got half a set of car keys in the morning over his Lucky Charms. The true key to the kingdom was to be delivered, along with tuition for driver's ed, on his actual birthday, in November.

But for tonight's party, Jake would have to rely on some cocktail of public transportation—bus, subway, bus, subway, subway, cab—although there was always the possibility that some other love-addled mom like Liz would drive him home. Liz herself was otherwise occupied. It was his job to figure it out.

As Liz watched him hunch over his breakfast (two bowls of cereal, a yogurt, *and* a peanut butter sandwich), it seemed to her that Jake had grown several inches in just those seven days. The curve of his back was so long. It was as if, suddenly, three extra vertebrae had been added to the staircase of his spine. These days, it often seemed to Liz that Jake grew before her eyes, like kudzu maybe, the way he had as an infant, when Richard, a still awe-stricken young father, used to take pictures of him as he slept, in an effort to document the phenomenon, as if Jake were Bigfoot or a UFO.

As for the other kid—Coco, her baby—she would require parental accompaniment to her midget soirée: a six-year-old's birthday, at the Plaza Hotel, no less; a sleepover! For Liz's whole life, prior to drinks in the Oak Room last year when Richard was interviewing for his gig at the university, she had been inside the Plaza only when she was in Midtown and in need of a public restroom. As Coco's designated lady-in-waiting, she saw tonight as her night to howl. This year Coco was in kindergarten for the second time, a condition of her admission to Wildwood Lower when they moved to the city. A private school. An apartment in Manhattan. The Plaza. Born and raised in the Bronx, in Co-op City, Liz couldn't always believe her new life.

In Ithaca, where they'd lived pretty fucking happily the last ten years—Richard and his meteoric rise at Cornell, Liz's dipping in and out of the Art History Department, the campus's dramatically stunning landscape, the low-key community vibe—irrepressible little Coco had been the life of the party. Here in New York, Coco was both a bad influence and intensely popular. In the last seven months she had had more invitations, and to swankier spots (boat rides around Manhattan, screenings at Soho House, grab-what-you-cans at Dylan's Candy Bar) than Liz had received in her entire lifetime.

Coco was one of three adopted Chinese daughters in her class—one of whom was also named Coco. Their Coco was now Coco B., the way Liz had been Elizabeth C. (née Cohen) all her grade-school life. The whole purpose of naming Coco "Coco" had been to avoid the initial, and yet there, like a wart at the end of a nose, it was. Poor Jake had been Jake B. so long and so often, in Ithaca, and now in New York, that some of the kids at Wildwood Upper had taken to calling him Jacoby—like those ambulance-chaser lawyers who, Liz was amazed to find, after all these years still ran their ads in the subways: "Hit by a truck? Call Jacoby and Meyers." (What if you just *felt* like you'd been hit by a truck? Liz wondered. What if you just *felt* like you'd been hit by a truck day after day? Could you call Jacoby and Meyers then?)

Tall, thin Jake was lanky now, with shoulders. Men's shoulders. When did he get such shoulders? Liz wondered, as he sidled past her to put his cereal bowl in the sink in the galley kitchen, where she was pouring her second cup of coffee. And then, when he brushed past her again, Liz resisted the urge to touch them. Instead, as he grabbed his backpack, called out, "Bye, guys," and hurried down the long, skinny hallway that led to the apartment's front door, she mentally dropped a dollar in the "shrink" jar, the imaginary fund she kept for the future therapy Jake would require as a result of her outsize adoration.

"Bye-bye, sweetie! Have a great day," Liz yelled down the hall.

"Hang tough, slugger," said Richard from the other room, perhaps ironically. One couldn't always tell.

Jake was rushing to meet his friends at the Ninety-sixth Street subway station and he apparently did not have time to kiss her goodbye. The commute was very convenient, although this would change when they moved again in the summer. Right now, Jake and a bunch of other Wildwood high schoolers from the Upper West Side schlepped up to the lush and lovely Riverdale campus en masse, and Liz was grateful he was part of a crowd. "I travel with the guys, Mom," he said, not in annoyance per se, but to reassure her, whenever Liz gave voice to some quasi-ridiculous worry. What if you get mugged? What if terrorists attack again?

In Ithaca, where they'd lived most of his life, Jake biked on his own from fourth grade onward, from school to Collegetown to Ithaca Falls. He'd take Ithaca transit, just like Nabokov had, whenever he ventured up the hill to meet Richard for lunch on campus, placing his little silver two-wheeler on the rack on the bus's front bumper alongside the big ones belonging to the college students and the earthier, crunchy professors (the ones who lived "off the grid"). In Ithaca, Jake had often been on his own, unless Liz was ferrying a Boy Scout troop full of his friends to the cool, blue stage of the lake for swim practice, and none of them, not Richard, not Jake, not Liz, had ever given this healthy independence a second thought.

Jake was fifteen and a half last Friday, which meant almost sixteen. As the door slammed behind him, that fact hit her, as it did every once in a while, out of the blue.

"Richard," Liz said, walking out into the hall, still in the old KISS T-shirt she liked to sleep in and her pajama bottoms. "Do you think that the way I feel about Jakey being a teenager is similar to what it's like to awaken from being drugged and find that an organ trafficker has stolen your kidney?"

"That's exactly what I was thinking," said Richard. He was standing in the living room, at the dining table he used as his desk, sorting through piles of papers, cutting a ridiculously handsome figure, Liz thought, for that hour of the morning. No matter the level of dishabille the rest of the household suffered—Liz sometimes wearing the T-shirt she'd slept in to take Coco to school—Richard looked *fine*: freshly shaven, crisp white shirt, sports coat, black jeans, green eyes bright, his silvering hair cut close to his well-formed head. Making order out of chaos.

Their apartment was a month-to-month sublease; the living

room was living, dining, and den, plus Richard's office, all rolled into one. The gleaming brand-new faculty housing the university had dangled in front of them, part of its full-blown Richard-recruitment package, wasn't completed yet.

"Coco and I will be going straight *to the Plaza* after pickup," Liz called out. She was back in the kitchen arranging Coco's meal. She said "to the Plaza" in a faux-snooty voice, both impressed and embarrassed by how impressed she was by the x factor of their evening. "After school, Jake will probably stay up in the Bronx anyway, so it's okay if you work late." As if Richard ever came home at a decent hour.

"He's not a kid anymore, Lizzie, he'll be fine," Richard said.

"He'll probably grab something to eat on Johnson Avenue, or hang out in a friend's basement waiting for the party to start," Liz said. She stood on tiptoe to reach the microwave oven and zapped the Tater Tots. Coco's hot breakfast.

Jake's party was in a mansion in the Fieldston section of the Bronx, that much Liz knew. Her son's Bronx was not her Bronx. "Marjorie says the party is definitely a chaperoned event, with parents ready and eager to taste-test the punch bowl." Liz had been assured this much over the phone the night before by her tenth-grade-class source, a fast-talking, well-meaning real estate agent mother.

"Deep Throat," Richard said, as she handed him the Tater Tots and a toaster waffle for Coco, who was already stuffing organic strawberries the size of golf balls into her exquisite little mouth.

"Deep Throat," Liz murmured. A nom de guerre in the mother wars. "Richard, that's perfect."

"Coco, how much do you think you cost me in strawberries

a year?" Richard asked. "These things are like six dollars a box and she must eat a box a day, right, Lizzie?"

"Daddy," said Coco, her wide smile pink with berry jam.

"At least one box," said Liz, "sometimes two, although thank God she's eating something not 'white food,'" she said.

"I eat not 'white food,'" said Coco.

"Bagels, pasta, waffles," said Liz, listing Coco's meals of choice. "Dumplings."

"Tater Tots," crowed Coco, picking one up in victory. "They're brown."

"Indeed they are," Richard said, cherry-picking the darker ones out of her hand and popping them into his own mouth.

He sort of listened now as Liz went on and on about her anxieties about the evening—What should I wear? "Hippie chic?" said Richard. Should we really be accepting such a lavish invitation? "Why not? It will be fun for both of you." It was part of their daily rhythm, him soothing her while glancing at the headlines of the *New York Times*. Every once in a while, Richard helped Coco with her "math" homework as well, by eating more of her Tater Tots. "Two minus one equals a very hungry Coco," said Richard, while assembling his breakfast shake at the other end of the table: bananas, peanut butter, protein powder, Matcha green tea—tea that "matchas your eyes," Liz told him when he first brought it home. He exuded competence. He was a self-cleaning oven. And even after all these years, Liz was not immune to the power of his good looks.

"One of the moms asked me to be on the Multicultural Festival committee for next fall—do you think I should?" asked Liz.

Wildwood prided itself on "diversity," which was one of the

reasons she and Richard had picked it last year. In Coco's class there were five other Asian girls, an African American boy, a West Indian boy with a lyrical lilt in his voice—Liz volunteered on class trips just to hear him speak—one tow-headed born-wearing-a-blazer WASP, and the rest a motley crew of half-Jewish kids. Like Jake.

"Might be a way to meet people," said Richard, nodding.

"Marjorie says, 'Sure there's diversity. There's millionaires . . . and then there's billionaires.' "

"I'm glad you've made a friend, honey," said Richard. As if it were possible that she might not have.

Marjorie was divorced and had suffered, and therefore was imbued with enough compassion to welcome in a newcomer. A tiny, wiry pinwheel of a person, she also lived on the Upper West Side, hence the affinity between the two mothers, and she'd been exporting her own kids to the Bronx to Wildwood for years, so she definitely had wisdom to share. Her twins were named Henry and James. Fraternal, they still looked an awful lot alike, although Henry was lankier and his features were finely etched, while James's face looked similar but thicker, as if it had been stretched by Silly Putty.

Henry, the nice twin, had become Jake's best friend in a New York minute. He was one of those kids who always had a broken arm. But soulful, Liz thought.

It was Henry who introduced Jake to McHenry, Davis, and Django. His "posse." Liz was relieved that Jake had so quickly made friends who could guide him through this foreign, urban terrain.

"Okay, Coco-bear, brush your teeth and grab your stuff,"

said Richard. It was one of the rare days he was taking her to school. He'd usually left for the office by this point, but because the girls were spending the night out, he was adding a half hour of quality time with his kid by escorting her on the morning commute.

Liz was standing like a sentry at the door, Coco's backpack in hand. "C'mon Coco," she called. "Get the lead out." She could hear the water in the bathroom sink running.

"What do you have up today?" asked Richard as he organized his briefcase.

"Yoga, food-shop, packing for tonight, bills, the car inspection, those stupid summer camp health forms . . . stuff," she listed a little defensively. There was plenty to do.

Coco came loping down the hall. "Bring my Chinese pajamas," she said as she offered her forehead to Liz for a goodbye smooch.

"You got it," Liz said. Then she leaned over to Richard. "Aren't you forgetting something?" She said this every morning, and once in a while, like today, elicited a less-than-abstracted kiss.

It was a pleasure to see them go, and to close the door behind them.

It was heaven really to be alone in that cramped apartment. And yet, as she had felt almost every day since they'd moved in, when she came back from dropping Coco off at school, or yoga, or errands, or coffee, Liz took one look at her messy home and was overwhelmed by how much there was to do and how little she wanted to do it. Finding that first step into an amorphous day, a day without bones, was always the hardest.

She walked over to her laptop. It was on the coffee table in front of the couch, where she'd left it late last night. She typed in "feigenbaum/blogspot.com."

Hours later, most of her tasks accomplished and tucked away behind her, Liz sat on Wildwood Lower's marble front steps with her old duffel and Coco's Barbie Overnight Bag resting between her knees, her head tilted back to capture the warmth of the spring sun. A yummy buttery light permeated her closed eyelids—all winter long she had craved this. The school was located in the East Nineties, between the smoky gray branches of trees that rimmed Central Park on Fifth Avenue and the bright yellow splashes of taxi traffic east on Madison. It was housed in a limestone fortress, a former home of some robber baron, probably destined to go to a hedge fund guy in the near future when the Wildwood capital campaign hit its mark and they broke ground on a new building. She was early for pickup, ever eager to find out if Coco's day had been thumbs-up or thumbs-down—it had been a roller-coaster transition to Manhattan life for all of them. Except Richard.

Although, through years of experience, Liz knew that if all the calm, focused energy he had displayed day in and day out these last few months were to be translated into a normal person's emotions, the result would actually look something like excitement and anxiety.

"They made you an offer you can't refuse," Liz had said, late some fragrant, sultry night the summer before, back in Ithaca, after they'd had sex, when they were sitting barefoot on their front porch drinking beers like kids, talking over the pros and cons of taking the job, their children safely asleep inside. It was obvious how much he'd wanted it.

"It's not the same city you grew up in," Richard had said, to reassure her.

It was a thought she'd held on to.

"Just think of all the museums and the galleries," he said.

He was right about that, Liz thought as she waited for Coco—the Upper East Side in this new moneyed century was not the New York she'd grown up in at all. Hyacinths in spun sugar colors bloomed in the window boxes of the town houses across the street. Cherry blossoms wept snowy petals in the breeze. The stoop she sat on was a far cry from the benches she'd hung out on in Section Five of Co-op City, the soulless middle-class housing project where Liz twisted in the winds of boredom during her own rather turbulent adolescence. All those concrete towers and windswept sidewalks, the outdoor shopping centers and indoor garages, the basketball courts without basketball nets, like chain-linked prison yards where the boys played shirts and skins all afternoon before feeling you up in some dank, stinky stairwell later that evening. The absolute dearth of trees. That hard, unyielding concrete universe that her adult world would determinedly negate and her children would not grow up in.

With her eyes closed, Liz could hear the chitchat chattering background hum of the other mothers, the way she used to hear the *ch-ch-ch* of the lawn sprinklers while she sat in her car by the curb across from the ball fields in Ithaca and waited for her offspring to explode out of school when the final bell rang.

Liz had loved all that: living in the country, the cocoon of her car with her music on. Teenagery stuff like Lucinda Williams. Yo-Yo

Ma and the music of Ennio Morricone from all those Sergio Leone spaghetti westerns—the CD finding its way into her Hanukkah stocking last year alongside a pretty carnelian red bangle with a little lump of ironic coal lodged in at the toe. Oh, the bennies and compromises of a mixed marriage! The cello had been so awesomely beautiful it seemed to actually bend her insides. She'd arrive early and park, just to savor the music a little longer, idling outside of Cayuga Heights Elementary after half-day nursery, or the Dewitt Middle School later in the afternoon, waiting for Jake post-soccer. In the passenger seat next to her always was a pack of healthy snacks—lady apples and cucumber slices, peanut butter and banana sandwiches on wooly bread—anticipating the kids' descent. Homemade. Local. Organic. (Well, the peanuts weren't local, but they'd been crushed into mush at the local food co-op; the bread was homemade there, too, homemade at the store.) This happy, lazy array of nourishing, nutritional foodstuffs made Liz feel maternal, nurturing, and beneficent, practically winged. That station wagon was like a little mobile home for her and the children: Mother Ginger and her skirts. She'd reveled in the privacy. That was life in Ithaca, and it did not suck.

Since the move, Liz spent her time mostly ferrying Coco around town, from Wildwood to occupational therapy to play dates to ballet class to Chinese school. What had happened to all the gallery hopping Richard had dangled as bait? Liz did more commuting here in the city than she'd ever done in Ithaca. Picking up and dropping off. Picking up and dropping off. It sounded like the lexicon of drug dealers.

Today at Wildwood Lower, like all days when it wasn't raining, the stay-at-homes gathered in little cliques for kindergarten pickup at their various stations along the sidewalk: the JAPs with the JAPs, the head-banded preppy moms with the preppies, the stray earth mother in Birkenstocks with a baby in a sling, singing softly to herself and swaying her hips to rock the baby to sleep.

Next on the food chain, the "caregivers": a couple of grad students reading Kierkegaard or Sartre and listening to their iPods; the pierced and tattooed European au pairs staring off into space, dreaming of a night in the dance clubs; and the small dark fortress of the Caribbean nannies, with their slow, sexy patois as they greeted one another on the opposite side of the staircase from the mothers, the two groups almost never commingling, a tale of two cities, two pickups.

Liz opened her eyes and saw a clutch of yummy mummies at the foot of the steps; she'd been part of this scene for only nine months but she knew queen bees when she saw them. They were tall in their metallic sandals; their skinny yoga butts trim in their designer jeans, their long, shiny, blown-out, streaked hair (Breck Girl hair, Liz thought, silently dating herself) flowing halfway down their backs in glossy sheets. Only experience told her that when these ladies turned away from their gabby circle to place a cell phone call to their driver or decorator or art consultant, that the skin on their faces would be pure leather. "It's just like high school," Liz wrote to her best friend, Stacey, in an email, "the scene at pickup. The blond girls. Everybody else. Me."

In the nine months her kids were at Wildwood, Upper and Lower, Liz had met literary agent mothers and banker mothers, cancer researcher mothers and former microbiologists; she'd met a lot of formers. Former lawyers and former investment bankers and former PR people. Wasn't she a former art historian herself?

The husbands worked too much and traveled too much—they were always in Mumbai opening up offices. They earned too much money for their wives to justify being away from the kids the long hours their former careers required. The "formers" made up the bulk of the PTA.

Case in point was Casey, Juliana's mom, the hostess of tonight's slumber party at the Plaza. Casey was the PTA president. She used to oversee concessions for all the Loews movie theaters in the country. A former concessionaire. Meanwhile, her husband, an ophthalmologic surgeon, was always flying around the globe heroically saving the sight of some corrupt third world leader.

The Plaza Hotel was going to be shut down for two years; a developer was remodeling it into condominiums. "It's our girls' last chance," Casey, mouth full of cheese cubes, had whispered into Liz's ear over warm white wine on curriculum night. It would be just three girls plus Juliana, three girls and their moms. "So don't tell anyone." Wildwood had a no-cut policy regarding birthday parties; it was simply verboten not to invite the entire class to absolutely everything. And preferably, the entire grade.

Juliana was a sweet kid, all button nose and sass and a sprinkling of cinnamon-colored freckles. The girls had had a few play dates, and Liz liked Juliana; she said her *please*s and *thank-you*s and, like Coco, was able to play on her own. Some of the kids Coco brought home required play instruction. They needed art projects or cookie baking or Build-A-Bear Workshop, Xbox, constant supervision. Sometimes, when Liz was exhausted and sick of writing the script of their activities, she'd resort to popping in a video, cracking a beer, and watching the girls zone.

Liz knew only one of the other kids attending the sleepover: Clementine, a small-boned, quiet, introspective sort with a cloak of long dark hair. The kind of girl who grows up to be a poet or to play the guitar in the high school yard off by herself at lunchtime, a certain kind of sensitive boy staring at her longingly, a boy, Liz thought, a lot like Jake.

Clementine was the kind of kid Liz would have made into her own best friend, mysterious and hard to reach, doling out the sweet satisfaction of breaking through to her, the pleasure in being chosen, anointed. But Clementine wasn't for Coco, the party animal. Coco would steamroll over all that subtlety.

The last guest was Juliana's best friend from preschool. "You'll like Marsha, the mother," said Casey. "She's very down-to-earth; the little girl's name is Kathy."

Although Liz had jawed on the phone about the party with Deep Throat Marjorie—the extravagance! The expense!—she was actually looking forward to this night. It had been kind of hard these last few months. Liz felt too old and specific now to make new friends, and except for Marjorie, she hadn't, really. Richard was right to worry. Midlife was like that. High school and college and grad school had been all about hanging out. Then there were work colleagues and cocktails. Babies meant hanging out again, too, long days in the playground, pizza suppers in the park by the lake. But now Liz was an astronaut traveling solo in her own little capsule, which was better sometimes than not, but still lonely. There were probably some people in New York she should look up—school pals; that couple they'd been so close to in D.C., when Richard and the wife both worked at the World Bank. But oddly, Liz hadn't had the appetite for it. Email had become an enabler, practically paralyzing her when it came to picking up the handheld, and yet she hadn't written her way back in touch with a whole lot of people, either. She was afraid that there was both far too much to catch up on and way too little to say. Liz's best friend lived in Marin, and over the years her relationship with Stacey had dwindled from hours on the phone to short staccato bursts of email, sometimes a week or two in between, though every so often there was a daily volley through cyberspace, two or three in a matter of minutes, as if they were engaging in honest-to-God conversation. Lately, Stacey had taken to Googling her old boyfriends and forwarding the results to Liz—a barrage of balding, fat oral surgeons. Liz kept emailing her back: "You dodged a bullet!" and "Count that baby's chins!" Email allowed her flexibility, a cruelty that could be whisked away and out of sight with the one-two punch of a double click.

In the last set of emails, Stacey had changed her tactics. She'd taken to Googling *Liz's* exes—maybe because she'd finally run out of her own. One, a "Writing from Experience" TA Liz had had a short, unhappy affair with as a freshman, produced the mother lode. Daniel Feigenbaum. This guy kept a blog, a cyber journal. Stacey sent her the link. Unbeknownst to anybody, including him—oh, the blessings of online obscurity—Liz had been tuning in every day for a month. Now she was as addicted to his blog as she'd been addicted to *General Hospital* in college. Most of it was boring stuff (his work, at an ad agency), some of it was painful (he still dreamed of becoming a novelist), some of it was embarrassingly enthralling (his sexual fantasies about transvestites). It was so intimate, being this close to Daniel Feigenbaum—closer than she'd ever been in real life, even when they'd lain naked together, skin to skin—that after a week or two Liz had felt sympathy for him, although in college he'd barely been nice to her. Booty calls, some retarded conversations about Thomas Pynchon, cashew chili dinners. And then when she'd fallen for someone who had actually wanted to date her and be her boyfriend, Daniel Feigenbaum had published a mean little story about her in the graduate literary magazine.

Surely if Liz were now to run into Daniel Feigenbaum in an airport or a grocery store after all these years, he wouldn't catch up with her by telling her about the tranny porn he downloaded regularly, if he even remembered her at all. Yet he posted all this info online, for the whole world to see. It was his choice. So why did she feel like she was crawling through his apartment window and rifling through his drawers? Trolling his diary entries—she'd gone back weeks and even months, sometimes in a single sitting— made her teeth ache, like when she'd eaten too much candy. Yet, over time, with all this intimate access to the inner workings of Daniel Feigenbaum's heart, she also found herself rooting for the home team. She wished for his success. Liz had yet to confess her newfound addiction to the Feigenbaum blog to Richard, who doubtlessly wouldn't care, or to Stacey, for that matter, who could sometimes cut to the core of what was wrong with her too quickly for her to bear. Maybe little Kathy's mom, this Marsha, would be someone easy to talk to—Liz could tell her the bare minimum of her cyber-sleuthing and they could laugh about Liz's idée fixe over tea. Liz had always wanted to stay at the Plaza. She'd had her Eloise fantasies, same as anyone.

"Busers exiting," announced Kevin, the red-haired, gray-jacketed, six-foot-six security guard, as maybe ten kids of differing heights and ages walked out of the school single file and were led by two assistant teachers to two waiting yellow minibuses. All the kids at school knew his exact height; they'd point up at him and holler, "He's six foot six." Kevin would smile tolerantly. The man was a mountain. He reminded Liz of one of those mozzarella pigs she'd seen hanging in the shops in Rome, his skin a little yellow and oily like a giant smoked cheese. On Halloween, he'd good-naturedly don an XXX-large version of the Lower School girls' pleated gray skirts; it was the size of a beach umbrella, his mammoth naked calves goose-bumped and hammy in the breeze.

As Kevin roared his edict, "Kindergarten pickup!" the clusters of waiting adults immediately began to merge, funneling like sand in an hourglass toward the two red doors where the children would exit the building class by class and line up in rows on the sidewalk. Liz stood and stretched, yanking up her low-slung jeans as she rose, and smoothing out the pretty embroidered Indian shirt—soft blue velvet with tiny mirrors—that she'd unearthed from her closet when she saw its exact facsimile hanging in a posh storefront window on Madison Avenue with a price tag of one zillion dollars. She felt pretty in that shirt. She'd felt pretty in it three decades ago. A miracle, still feeling pretty. She twisted her long brown hair into a loose knot, swung her duffel over her shoulder; Coco's Barbie bag came with wheels and could be dragged along the sidewalk like a poodle toy.

Coco wouldn't have been caught dead in a party dress, so Liz had folded up some leggings and a tie-dyed mini, a couple of different T-shirts to choose from: Happy Bunny, Cocoa Puffs, Paul Frank's Monkey Julius—the one where the toothy ape was wearing braces—plus the requested Chinese pajamas, and packed

them in her bag. The children in the Lower School wore uni-
forms, that is, a solid pant (not jeans) or said pleated skirt and a
white polo shirt. A plain gray cardigan sweater with the school's
logo stitched into the corner in a silvery thread. Coco would be
tearing hers off halfway down the block, throwing it over her
shoulder in a wadded-up ball, confident that her mother would
be there behind her to catch it. She'd pull a white leather news-
boy cap—she loved that cap! (but Mrs. Livingston said no caps
in school)—out of the backpack that Liz's older sister, Michelle,
had sent from Italy for Coco's last birthday. She was particularly
prone to the latest fads, Coco. Liz could only hope that tattooing
and scarification would no longer be de rigueur when Coco was
old enough to self-mutilate.

Liz felt a light hand on her shoulder and turned around. Casey.
Same freckled face and shoulder-length reddish curls as Juliana.
Hollow cheeks. Tired eyes. She'd probably been pretty cute as a
girl, but now she looked prematurely old and too skinny. It's your
butt or your face—you can't have both, Liz thought. Some movie
star had said this; she'd read it or heard something like it somewhere, and had stored a smudged replica of the quote in the hash
of celebrity trivia her brain had accumulated without effort, along
with all the other stuff and nonsense that passed for knowledge
these days from print magazines and whatever: TV, the Net, idle
chitchat, the air . . . But it was true, about your butt or your face.

"I see you've brought your bags . . . Please don't tell anyone,
Liz . . ."

"I won't, I won't," Liz said, in response to Casey's stricken expression. "I'll just say we're going away for the night." As if anyone
would ask, anyway. They all took off for somewhere every week-

end, limos destined for Teterboro Airport clogging the street in front of the school, Hummers with Connecticut plates lining up at the curb. Nobody here would notice Liz's little overnight bags.

"You look like a teenager," Casey said, approvingly, taking in Liz's jeans and blouse, the platform clogs she'd walked across the park in, her soft, messy knot of hair. "You look like a teenager from behind." And then: "Isn't that Coco B. getting chewed out by Mrs. Livingston again?"

Of course it was Coco B. Liz didn't even have to turn around to know.

"Oh no," she said, feigning . . . fear? Surprise? Disappointment? Whatever it was a proper mother was supposed to feel, aside from resignation and a little residual renegade thrill. The truth was, Mrs. Livingston, in her flesh-colored stockings and Pappagallo flats, inspired juvenile delinquency: whenever Liz was called into school to meet with her, she had the urge to go to the ladies' room first and light up a cigarette. She'd even smoked a little weed in Central Park before the last parent-teacher conference. Richard chewed her out after that meeting was over. He said he hoped he was the only one who'd noticed her red rims.

But half the moms were zoned on Xanax anyway and the other half had foreheads that didn't move, so even if they were emoting, they looked like zombies. Mrs. Livingston was surely used to checked-out mothers, Liz had assured Richard. She was no better or worse than most of them—which was really the secret of life, her life, Liz had decided at that moment, while she was still stoned: she was neither better nor worse than most. The ones with the frozen foreheads, there was always a little curl of flesh near the hairline that the dermatologist forgot to paralyze. When the mothers got excited it would roll up toward their roots, like an awning.

There she was now, Mrs. Livingston, her ropey hand firmly on Coco's chin, forcing Coco to stare back at her. "Show me your eyes" was a favorite tool of Mrs. Livingston's, a vote-with-your-feet proponent of pediatric hypnotism.

"Uh-oh," said Liz. A little too halfheartedly. Lamely enough to elicit a quizzical stare.

"We'll meet you later at the hotel," said Casey, with cool curiosity. "We have to go home first to get our bags anyway."

"Sounds good," said Liz, pushing through the crowd toward her daughter. And then, over her shoulder, as a polite afterthought: "We're so looking forward to it." This was clearly the wrong thing to say, for Casey shot her a look of pure hatred.

Liz fought her way through the various coteries toward Coco, the big kids lining up in front of the Mister Softee truck waiting for ice cream, mothers using their shopping bags like mountain dogs to shepherd their offspring and play dates past the vacant-eyed Mexican balloon seller from whom Liz had never, not once, seen anyone buy anything. There she was, *anxious* Liz!—now more eager to get to her delinquent kid. She could spy through the crowds Mrs. Livingston holding Coco by both shoulders in a teacherly death grip. So Liz pushed on through the hugging, scolding, shooing, Italian-ice-buying throngs. She bypassed boys on scooters and girls skating on their Heelys, navigating a Fellini film's worth of activity, and still managing to nod a worried hello to the occasional father in a business suit (determined to get an early start to "the country") and to the coaxing, nagging nannies proffering donuts in outstretched hands, luring the miniature circus ponies home. Like a suicidal salmon, Liz swam relentlessly upstream to claim her daughter.

When they finally arrived at the hotel—a mildly chastened Coco and her thoroughly castigated guardian—it took a moment to spy the three little girls and their mothers in the pink, frondy Palm Garden, hidden behind the harpist. The girls were balancing on their knees on the Louis XIV chairs, using their thumbs to lick whipped cream off their plates, while the ladies picked at the remainders of their tea sandwiches at a neighboring table. Above them, palm trees soared like giraffe parasols, all long necks and sporadic splayed leaves. There were little potted pink azaleas in marble urns throughout the room, lending the inhabitants a youthful, rosy glow, even the smattering of Park Avenue dowagers and a rather large, boisterous group of women of a certain age, all wearing red hats and purple dresses. At the girls' table, Juliana was sporting an Egyptian collar of Mardi Gras beads and a feather boa; Clementine, the future poet, was staring dreamily at the harpist; and a little blonde Liz assumed was Kathy was sorting through a pile of geegaws and feathers. Coco took one look at the booty and hightailed it over there, left hand already outstretched, reaching for the gold.

At the grown-up table, directly below a huge, glittery chandelier, Casey was inclining her head toward Sydney, Clementine's mother, a tall, angular woman with attenuated features and a long, narrow, wedge-shaped head. With her closely cropped dark hair and wide-set ears, she looked like a purebred Siamese cat, sleek in her black cashmere leggings and feather-light sweater. The woman who must have been Liz's new best friend, Marsha, sat on Casey's other side, slathering clotted cream and jam on the remainder of a scone. She had shoulder-length center-parted brown hair, and wore mom jeans; she had already begun to let herself go. Why was Liz surprised? Casey had described her as "down-to-earth." Parenthood made strange bedfellows—there was no other moment in time that these four women would ever have spent an entire evening together. Yet, there was a happy buzz to the group, thank God. Liz could feel its vibrato as she approached. All that sugar, plus what looked like two bottles of champagne still sweating in their ice buckets next to the table, had created a lovely cloud of conviviality.

"Hey, ladies," Liz said, stepping in, it seemed, on the heels of what must have been the punch line of something hilarious.

The mommies looked up from their laughter with just-woken-up surprise. Perhaps they'd forgotten that Liz and Coco were joining them.

"What did that old bitch have to say?" asked Casey, by dint of greeting. She had the happy, drunken sheen in her eyes, like a coat of clear nail polish smeared across her blue irises, of a hostess at a successful party.

"She sent us to see Jane Perskey," Liz said.

Liz and Coco had spent a half hour waiting on an old blue velvet sofa outside the headmistress's office and a half hour on the newish burgundy velveteen sofa inside the office staring at the headmistress's porcelain pig collection. "I've never seen so many pig tchotchkes in my life."

"Oh my God," gasped Casey. "We sent Jane a Limoges pig when we were trying to get Jules into the school. As a Christmas bribe. She had it returned to us that very day, with a firm no-thank-you note. It came by car and driver. I was mortified, but they took Jules anyway." Casey sipped her champagne. "We were lucky. Juliana ERB'd off the charts, and my husband is a legacy. They had to take her." The ERB: the Educational Records Bureau exam kids took to qualify for kindergarten admissions. Luckily, the university had lent a hand in finding spaces for both Liz's kids and paying their tuition—it was almost impossible to get into these schools without pull. Marjorie had told Liz this much. That she was lucky. But it was evident.

"She got called into Perskey?" Sydney said, laughing. "Good for her. She must have transgressed royally to get inside the inner sanctum."

Well, yes. This time Coco had displayed such an outstanding array of bad behavior, a virtual peacock's tail of criminal activity, that Mrs. Livingston had washed her hands of her and sent Coco to the principal's office. So much for progressive education.

Or rather, so much for *the synthesis of the very best of progressive and traditional pedagogy as manifested by the Wildwood Plan*, Liz thought.

Here was today's list of transgressions: (1) Coco had pushed another girl by accident (maybe) down the stairs on her hell-bent journey to gym, resulting in blood (both elbows); (2) she'd started a water fight in the *boys'* bathroom; but, worst of all, (3) at the end of the day, during free time, she'd hopped up onto Mrs. Livingston's desk in the front of the classroom and said, "Nobody play with Juliana." That's right, the birthday girl, and their hostess for the evening, the one whose mother—thanks to the health insurance plans of several third-world dictators—was footing the hotel bill. Why would Coco B. do such a thing?

Liz asked her this (sans the initial) in front of the somewhat bemused, seen-it-all headmistress, Jane (that the teacher was addressed as Mrs. and the headmistress by her first name was just another example of Wildwood's nuanced eclecticism). Apparently Juliana had cheated in musical chairs. According to Coco—Coco with her heightened sense of social justice—cheating was for cheaters, especially when Coco didn't win.

"But she's the birthday girl," Liz said. "Coco, you don't ostracize a kid on her birthday."

It was decided that Coco would write Juliana a letter of apology that she could mail through the school's post office—a unit that effectively combined mathematics, art, and the social sciences, and was a perfect method of keeping track of who was popular and who wasn't by charting the number of letters sent and received, so it was also a unit on statistics. The fact that Coco knew only half her letters, and the ones she could accurately identify were often formed facing the wrong direction or sleeping on their tummies, didn't matter. She could use kindergarten spelling, said Jane. Even with this caveat, the whole endeavor would take hours of their weekend time at home. Coco hated to sit. She hated to write. She loathed apologizing. All this clucking and coaxing, back and forth between Liz and seen-it-all Jane—they sounded like a dovecote of cooing birds, a scripted dovecote—plus Liz's feeble attempts at being smart and funny and supportive in front of a discerning audience, and trying to appear publicly and sufficiently horrified by her daughter's errant behavior when she secretly found it sort of humorous, was finally enervating. By the time they left Casa Jane (that's what the enamel hand-painted sign outside of Jane's office read; when pressed, she admitted to winning it in a dance contest at Club Med Turks and Caicos after her divorce), Liz needed a martini.

How lucky she was that she was now regaling a bunch of drunken mothers with her tales out of school at the Palm Court of the Plaza Hotel, where it was easy enough to procure a drink. Grey Goose, heavy on the olives. Which Liz would ask for, as soon as she could grab the waiter's attention. After glancing furtively at the kids' table—Juliana and Coco were performing a charming tango together to the angel-winged rustlings of the harp—she sank back in her chair in relief, for it didn't seem that Juliana held any of Coco's misbehaviors against her. She was a good kid, Juliana.

Sydney called the waiter over. "Enrique, could you get our friend Liz here a drink?" And then quietly to Liz, "Honey, you look like you could use one."

Liz mouthed a silent thank-you.

"My pleasure, madam," said Enrique, an elderly man in uniform, who possessed a studied European elegance.

"He loves us," Casey whispered loudly. "We had two tins of caviar before you got here." And then, "Do you like caviar? I can order another."

"I could eat ten more of these scones," said Marsha. "But I shouldn't."

"No, no, but thank you," said Liz. "I just need alcohol, preferably intravenously."

"We can always have more sent up to the room," said Casey. "Caviar. Champagne. My husband called from Dubai this morning and told me to go crazy. He said, 'What the hell, enjoy yourselves; we're not throwing a bat mitzvah.'" She laughed.

"Oh my God," said Sydney. "I have four kids in Hebrew school. I'm planning on robbing a bank. I've even joined the celebrations committee . . . so we all don't book conflicting dates. With my oldest daughter, we had to register her party in the fourth grade; that's three years in advance." She drained her glass. She lifted it and said, "Champagne me," and Casey, laughing, emptied the last inch or two from both bottles into Sydney's flute.

Liz reclined on the pink Louis XIV chair across from the harpist in her flowing gown, next to a gilt-edged marble column beneath the tall palm trees and potted pink azaleas, and began to feel like a human being. Here in the pretty hotel lobby, her daughter pleasantly occupied, her husband and son out of sight and out of mind, it was almost as if she were on vacation—away, away, in a resort somewhere. Where, who knew? Palm Beach? There was something old-ladyish about this place, in an appealing way. It was the job-well-done, now-you-can-relax-in-a-hammock-of-sea-breezes-and-social-graces ambience. The idyllic pink flamingo'd Florida of her soul.

Enrique returned with the fixings for Liz's drink on a tray and it looked so good—little pearls of condensation dripping down the sides of the elegant silver shaker, proof positive of the icy cold elixir inside—that she almost wept. The martini was expertly shaken and poured, and it perfectly met the edge of the glass. Liz had to hover like a hummingbird over it to take that first welcome sip. From that angle she noticed that the carpet was fraying. As she raised her eyes to sea level she saw that Enrique's uniform was faded. Even the harpist's skin looked worn under her pancake makeup. Sydney's pink satin seat cushion sported a few shiny stains. Looking up, she saw that the leaves of the sun-deprived palm trees were dotted with urban blight.

They were shutting down the hotel. It had been neglected and had gone to seed. The pleasures it had once provided were being chipped away by the ticking clock. For a few giddy moments, she had forgotten why they were there. Something was ending.

"This is delicious, Enrique, thank you," she said. "How much longer will the hotel be open?

"We close soon," he said. "Nobody knows for sure."

"That's so sad," said Marsha.

"I've worked here thirty-five years," said Enrique, his dark eyes liquid and wide. "They say they will bring the Palm Court back, but once it is gone . . ."

The ladies looked at him. No one knew exactly what to say.

"Oh, sure they can!" said nice Marsha. "Perhaps it'll be even better. New and improved, you know?"

"Two years is a long time to wait for work," said Enrique. "They want me to take early retirement. But I'm not sure . . ." With the look of a man who had violated his own sense of dignity, he shrugged. "What can you do?"

Another beat of silence.

"Drink," said Casey, in nervous hostess mode, clearly anxious to dispel the gloom. "Enrique, please bring us another bottle." Then, with a flirty smile: "This time with an extra glass for you."

"In that case, I bring two," said Enrique.

And the ladies laughed.

• • •

It was five a.m. and Liz couldn't sleep. She couldn't sleep because Coco couldn't sleep. She was too wired from all the room service—chicken tenders and brownie sundaes, all that fat and sugar and artificial everything making her tawny skin glow orange and her diminutive aura buzz—and Liz, poisoned as well, grown-up poisoned, was hungover and crashing, so dehydrated her tongue felt like parchment paper she had to peel off the roof of her mouth. She hadn't drunk this much, she thought, since high school.

Mother and daughter had been sprawled out side by side on the king-size bed watching videos for hours. This newest period of respite came after an initial phase of screen time, from eleven p.m. to three a.m., when Coco was mostly jumping on the bed and Liz was curled up in a fetal position on the carpet. Progress has been made, Liz thought. It was a thought that comforted her. She had now crawled her way up off the floor and onto the bed; she was presently sitting up, sort of, her head and neck leaning against the headboard at a bizarre, but not nauseating, angle. It was five o'clock in the morning. It said so on the digital clock's glowing green dial, and the numbers echoed with a sick-making pulse on her inner lids when she shut her eyes, so she knew that this was true.

Luckily, each mother-daughter team had been assigned its own bedroom in the "Tony Soprano Suite," which Casey had rented, she'd said, for a song. It wasn't actually called the Tony Soprano Suite, of course, but that is how Sydney referred to it when they first swung open the doors, and since then, that's how

Liz thought of it. Because they each had their own rooms, Liz was
able to keep the door shut and the volume down at the Bergamot
end of the hall, enough to allow the other ladies and their daughters a little shut-eye. Marsha and Kathy were one door down;
Clementine and Sydney, the next bedroom over. All three rooms
overlooked Fifth Avenue and the little plaza with the fountain in it
at the entrance to the hotel—the Plaza's plaza. Then, at the corner
of Fifty-ninth Street, the suite and the hotel both hung a left and
the hall opened up into a massive L-shaped living room, half
of which overlooked Central Park. A long, ornate dining room
glided along Fifty-ninth Street heading toward Sixth Avenue, followed by the master bedroom and bath, all with large windows
with picture-perfect park views, like grand landscapes hanging
in a gallery. This central part of the suite looked exactly like the
one Tony Soprano had once rented in a dream sequence, Sydney
swore to it (Liz had never seen the show; motherhood had robbed
her of her taste for violence), and Liz believed her. It was thickly
overdone. All gilt and gold, the chandeliers simply ridiculous,
and the furniture overstuffed. The bathroom in the main bedroom—Juliana and Casey's—was a two-unit affair: double sink,
toilet, shower, and bidet in a room the size of a studio apartment;
and in the other, an enormous tub was raised up on a marble stage
like a giant cake stand. It faced a floor-to-ceiling glass window
that, of course, overlooked the park. The ceiling of this bathtub
room was domed and adorned by a rococo extravaganza of fat
little painted cherubim. At one point in the evening, all the real
little cherubim had ended up in this Jacuzzi together, first with
their clothes on and then naked, dressed only in soap bubbles—
all at Coco's behest.

But first came the pedicures.

"We don't pay those Korean women enough," Sydney had said with a little wink at Liz, rising to her feet and passing the petal pink polish to Marsha. It had been a rollicking evening. The mothers swapped sex stories while the little girls gave each other makeovers, heavy on the eye makeup, until they looked like miniature Russian whores. It was at some point after that that Coco had managed to get them all, even the reticent Clementine, into the giant tub, into which she had poured all the in-house bubble bath. All this decadent beauty reminded Liz of the sprites at the Allée d'Eau, at Versailles, the wet, shiny, prepubescent girls flipping and flopping among the bubbles like baby seals, their mothers ringed around the bathroom sipping their champagne and wondering when exactly their own youth had abandoned them.

Then there'd been the pay-per-view movies—kid stuff for the kids—and more mommy talk. It turned out that Sydney had been a campaign consultant in her former incarnation. "Nobody who ever won," she said, dryly. "Gary Hart, talk about the winner's touch." But still, thought Liz, that must have been exciting. "That must have been exciting," she said, and Sydney's eyes misted for a moment. "It *was* really fun," she said, "the camaraderie, the sense of purpose. It was sort of great to have a mission . . . but I got married, I had kids," and here she leaned over—her shy little girl was sitting on the floor with the rest of the kids watching *Herbie Fully Loaded*—and lovingly gathered Clementine's hair into a shiny ponytail, wrapping it around and around her fist. "Now the four of them are my mission," Sydney said, giving Clementine's head a little kiss before releasing the long silky locks in an uncoiling twist, and Liz noted, not for the first time, that someday little Clementine would be a great beauty.

The women talked and talked. They talked about the schools, the camps, the real estate, until Liz thought her head would shoot off her neck, and then, one by one, the girls faded. Like tulips on fragile stalks, they began to bend and nod on the couches in the living area until their grateful mothers carried them off to bed. It was so hard to be with other people, it was hard on everyone, be they social creatures or not; it was such a relief to retire into seclusion, the bacchanal officially over. That is, all except for Coco, who seemed to grow more wound up and animated the more exhausted she became.

Now it was five o'clock in the morning, and Coco still did not sleep.

"When I was a child, there was no twenty-four-hour Cartoon Network," said Liz, but Coco couldn't have cared less. There was one now.

"Let's turn it off for a while," Liz said, with a little moan. She flipped over too fast and her brain sloshed from side to side within her skull, like water in a sinking rowboat in the middle of a rough, turbulent sea.

"What will we do now, Momma?" asked Coco.

Sleep, thought Liz. We could sleep. "Coco, we could sleep, baby," she said.

"I'm not tired," said Coco. She didn't look like she was. Her black eyes were shining. Her skin was the delicious caramelized brown of a butterscotch cookie. She was a great-looking kid. Her birth mother must have been gorgeous. Liz wished she could send her a postcard, right here, right now, with Coco's picture on it.

Liz hoped it would give her comfort. The desperate woman, who had left newborn Coco in the orphanage doorway in a threadbare nightie, umbilicus still attached, wrapped in newspapers to keep her warm.

"What time is it?" asked Liz rhetorically, for she was peering at her wristwatch. "Maybe it's sunrise time. Coco Louise Mei Ping Bergamot, have you ever seen the sun rise?"

Coco shook her head no, she never had.

"Come, we have to tiptoe, *shh, shh*, quietly," said Liz and she hoisted herself up on one elbow and then swung her legs over the side of the bed. When she stood, the floor made a rocking motion, in accompaniment to her head, a little like a bongo board before it steadied.

"*Shh*, Coco, come," said Liz.

"I didn't say anything," said Coco, running to her mother and taking her hand.

"Don't breathe, baby," Liz said.

They tiptoed down the carpeted, dark hall. They made their way into the living room. Streetlights lit up the park below. Liz sat herself in the window seat, and Coco climbed up into her lap.

Below, the park was dark green velvet with jeweled stitching, streetlights strung along the roads. As they watched, a wave of gray light—dawn, it must be *the* gray light of dawn, Liz thought—passed over Fifth Avenue and began to spread across the park. Soon half the park was lit, the smoky dark luminescence of morning, and the other half was still inversely radiant with the green-black nothingness of night. Liz had never seen anything like it.

"It's half morning," said Coco.

"Yes, sweetie pie," said Liz.

The light made its steady progression from east to west, and soon the whole park was illuminated by the ashy-dusky light, and then the sky turned pink; it turned pink in increments, a great pink wave rolling across the park, and on its back rode a large white hawk.

"It's a hawk," said Liz excitedly. "Coco, look! Maybe it's Pale Male."

Perhaps it was. Perhaps it was the famous red-tailed hawk who had made his nest on the outside of a fancy building on Fifth Avenue. Liz loved that hawk. He defied the urban forest of buildings and the cement skin that choked and encased the earth, building his little family a home where he damn well pleased. He'd even defied the wealthy, powerful residents of the building— Manhattanites!—with their co-op board battles and their warring lawyers and their positive and negative media exposure, and their spin; all those big guns called to arms over one lone hawk and his mate, some demanding he be turned out, then ripping down his nest, then delighting those who'd championed him by rebuilding it after all that bad press.

The brave, defiant hawk flew in great swoops over the park.

"Or maybe it's a pigeon, Momma," said Coco. "It's awfully small."

Yes, maybe it was. Liz kissed Coco on the back of her neck, directly on top of the tiny cigarette burn inscribed in her creamy skin like a little signature of ownership. Not every Chinese infant in their group of adoptive American parents was thusly scarred. The interpreter who had accompanied them to the orphanage had said at the time that scars like Coco's were there to be read like personalized tattoos, not designed to help the Chinese birth mothers identify their offspring in the future, as Liz and the other adoptive parents had first worriedly surmised, but rather as missives to whoever might find the little ones, that no matter what terrible set of circumstances had forced *this* woman to relinquish *this* baby, she still claimed her, marking her forever as her child.

By the time Liz got Coco home that morning—screw Saturday ballet and West African dance class; they were a schlep-and-a-half every weekend anyway—the kid was practically in a coma. She fell asleep during the cab ride home and Liz had to hold her under her arms with one hand, while jostling their overnight bags with the other, and walk her like Frankenstein's monster into their building. Coco never fully woke up. "*Now* you're asleep," Liz muttered under her breath. When they got into the apartment, Liz dragged Coco into her room and slung her across the bed. Her own mouth felt raw, as if she'd smoked a thousand cigarettes. Her body stank; alcohol was leaking out of her pores, although she'd bathed in that beautiful marble hotel shower ninety minutes before. The water had been so hot, and the soap had smelled so expensive and so good. She'd felt so clean!

There was no denying it, not in the moment nor later in guilty hindsight. Liz was a cranky, disheveled, hungover person when she walked back into her kitchen to make coffee. She was a person who wasn't sure if she'd just spent the evening before giving her young daughter a fairy-tale night to remember or if she'd ruinously inflated the kid's expectations for life. She was a person who, if you'd put a gun to her head at that moment, wouldn't have been able to recall the subtitle to her own dissertation. The title was "Modernism in Flight," that much she knew. She'd struggled mightily over it, worried at the time that she might box herself into one academic category or another, when her interests and passions were numerous. It was an art historian's study of the set and costume designs of the Ballets Russes. Liz had received her PhD in "modern thought." At the time, her dissertation had distinguished itself because she'd focused on the synthesis of art, design, and dance in a new and radical way. But now she couldn't remember the subtitle. For some reason this very question had popped into her mind during the cab ride home. What was it? She couldn't remember. She couldn't remember the opening line. She was struggling with this, she was struggling to remember the opening line to the dissertation she herself had written so many years before, so many lifetimes ago it felt like whatever it was she had written back then must have come out of someone else's mind, a mind that had been siphoned out of her body, leaving the scaffolding behind. She simply wasn't in mom-mode that morning. She felt done with all that; she'd had enough. Liz's antennae regrettably were not up.

Not up at all.

Jake entered the room just as she put the teapot on the stove to boil. He was still in last night's Coldplay T-shirt and his flannel pajama pants. They were too short. She'd bought them long five weeks before, but his newly hairy ankles were now poking out the bottom. So he'd made it home in one piece. He hadn't needed her. He was fine.

"Did you have a good time last night?" she asked him, as he opened the refrigerator and scanned its insides.

She could see the wings of his shoulder blades through his

T-shirt. She could see the bicep of his right arm flex as he held the refrigerator door wide open, letting all the cool air pour out. Jake was a beautiful boy, growing too fast, with hairy ankles, and she loved him. Probably she loved him too much. He'd told her that once when he was small. "Really, Jake?" she had said. "I really love you too much?" He'd noted her pain, he always noted it—she was unfair like that—and he said, "Too much love is better than enough." Taking pity on her. She loved him too much, but she could not think about him now.

"Yeah, I guess so," Jake said, as he lifted out the milk gallon and brought it to his lips. "I guess I had a good time, yeah." There was a little red string with some beads on it wrapped around his wrist. It looked silly, like something Coco might wear, but maybe not.

Liz didn't have the strength to yell at him. Shut the door. Don't waste energy. Use a glass! She didn't have the wherewithal to question his noncommittal answer. She turned off the gas under the kettle, reconsidering whether she would be able to tolerate the whistle. That stupid French press. What she wouldn't give for a Mr. Coffee now.

Jake took a long slug of milk and put the container back inside. He turned to her then, this boy, her boy; he looked straight at her, his green eyes burning with something. Humiliation? Anxiety? Confusion? There was bait there, but she did not rise.

He did not say, "Hey, Mom, can I talk to you about something?" He did not sit down at the table and wait for her to sit down next to him, all motherly concern and skill, to carefully draw whatever it was out of him, as she had done so many times before. None of these things happened.

Instead, Liz said, "All right, then, Mom's got a hangover," and sidled past him.

"Way to go, Mom," Jake said, in a voice that was at the same time too soft and still too hearty, like white bread with too many additives in it. But she didn't notice, she didn't notice until she examined and reexamined the whole morning under a microscope in retrospect, and she made her way into her bedroom to sleep off Coco's party. The bed was made, of course. That motherfucker, perfect Richard, had perfectly made it. Liz unmade it, pulled off her pants, unhooked her bra, and slid it out of one of her shirt-sleeves like she used to do at sleepovers or that one summer she went to camp. Then she slipped her body between the covers, which were cool and tightly bound to the bed. Richard was probably already at the office—where else would he have gone? He'd probably run a million laps around the reservoir, showered, changed, and headed uptown to his office like he did every single Saturday morning since they'd moved here.

Last night, both of Elizabeth Bergamot's children had had parties to go to. Bad mother Liz! She'd chaperoned the wrong one. She was going to mommy prison. Literally, she was.

· · ·

———————

T HERE WAS A GIRL he *liked* liked. Her name was Audrey.

Audrey was in his grade, but as with almost everyone else at school, she was older. She had short, sleek, dark hair, thick and lustrous, black as an oil slick. It dripped perfectly down around her perfect head, like a shiny onyx globe. Audrey's hair was cut so that it hung straight and glossy and curled under just at the tips of her earlobes, like two commas, strangely sexual, tiny clefts; it was that little swing that made it girl's hair, not boy's hair, and it was the swing—more of a sway, really, an undulation, *a quaver*—that drove Jake crazy.

Jake thought Audrey's haircut made her look French, although he had no idea really what that meant—he'd been to Italy a bunch of times, but not to France; he had an aunt who lived there, in Rome. When he went to Italy he liked to pretend he was Italian; he liked to eat a lot, and the food was *so* good. His aunt Michelle would let him drink wine and ride around on her Vespa, which drove his mother nuts. Audrey was Chinese, like his sister. Which was why she was old for their grade; most of the foreign-born adopted kids ended up old for their grade, while Jake was young to begin with, young at least for the city. He overheard his best friend Henry's mom say to his own mother one night: "In New York, we keep boys in preschool until they're shaving." The two women had been gabbing together over a glass of wine at Jake's house. They were a little looped. Mom-looped. Henry had been there, too; his mom had stopped by ostensibly to drag him home, and he'd been rolling his eyes at Jake over both their moms' heads all evening, because it was his mom, not Henry, who kept on staying. Henry's mom, Marjorie, had poured herself another round and gone on to imitate her kids' preschool ex–missions director through pursed lips: " 'Truth be told, boys this age are a bit Neanderthal. To get them into a first-tier kindergarten, we must wait until their neurological systems have had a chance to mature.' " This cracked Jake's mom up. The whole scene made Jake's mom laugh, except when it made her shake her head. But then she seemed lonely these days and had been drinking wine, so almost anything could elicit either response, and Henry's mom *was* funny. (In his mind's eye, when Jake heard the term "ex–missions director," he had imagined a little redbrick schoolhouse emitting a chain of small children in a series of puffs—like smoke rings— up into the sky through the chimney while some old lady stood outside cracking a whip.)

When Jake confided to Henry the French part, the part about Audrey looking French, *not the liking-her part*, when he said in a quiet voice as they passed her in the hallway one day after lunch that there was something about Audrey Rosenberg that seemed a little bit French, Henry whistled low and then whispered in Jake's ear with hot Dorito breath, *"Chinois."*

Jake Googled the word later, after school, when he was home alone, in his room with the door shut. It meant some kind of cookware, but it was also the French term for "Chinese," and it was the name of a restaurant in Las Vegas. Jake couldn't decide if the use of this word—whispered in the hall at school in a cloud of toxic orange cheesy dust—was hard-core evidence of Henry's ingrained sophistication or absolutely the complete opposite. *Chinois.* That was the problem and the intrigue of Henry as a best friend—the dialectical imbalance of sophistication and its opposite, *dialectical* also being a word of Henry's. But Jake liked words, which was part of why he liked Henry so much. They *used* words together when they talked, and words almost became their secret language, because they didn't sound like all the others. But *Chinois.* The feel of the lexeme unspoken in his mouth suited Audrey. (*Lexeme* was Jake's word; he'd looked it up, when he was sick of the word *word* for all the glittery multifaceted, polished gems that he and Henry excavated from the broken surface of the concrete world, now on an almost daily basis, in a kind of tournament of kindred spirits and my-dick-is-bigger-than-thou's.) *Chinois.* Exotic, diaphanous, *erotic*—another of Henry's favorites, as in "that babe is *e-ro-tic*," as he chose to refer to any girl in a too-short skirt. There was nothing sluttish about the word *Chinois.* It seemed sort of upper-class. Sensual. Concupiscent. Whatever it was, it was the right word for Audrey.

Most of the kids in Jake's grade traveled in groups. Like they had in Ithaca. Like they probably did everywhere, throughout history, throughout time. His mother said it was just that way when she was a kid, too. Like on TV or in the movies. Jocks with jocks, stoners with stoners, kids in bands, robotics geeks, chess nerds, some intermingling of the various categories—because these kids also prided themselves on their grades, their after-school stuff, teams and instruments and theater and politics and volunteering; they all volunteered or invented stuff scientifically; they spoke Chinese, but Jake didn't and his sister was. Jake's mother made her study Mandarin, but no one else in the family spoke a word of it, not even enough to order in a restaurant. The kids at school who didn't speak Chinese spoke Japanese or Hebrew, or they studied Latin and ancient Greek. Jake took Spanish. His dad was from California, and all his cousins on his dad's side were in Spanish-immersion programs; he took it so they could talk to each other at Christmas, behind their parents' backs.

There were very few couples at his school. Kids hooked up all the time, at parties, between classes, in cars or on the campus grounds, in the woods. They weren't in couples, though, mostly; they did not "go out." But Audrey was part of a couple; her boyfriend's name was Luke, and sometimes they would walk through the Humanities Building at school holding hands, or Luke would steer her by her elbow through the swarms of students like she was under arrest or something, or he'd grab her by her wrist and pull her along like a kite—she was so light she looked like she might lift off the ground. It was almost as if Audrey had to take little leaps just to keep up with him—maybe that's why she wore those shoes every day in the spring, those little gold ballet slippers, so she could skim the ground, two quick elastic steps, a double dash to Luke's single stride. In the winter she wore pink UGGs ironically, as if they were a joke, and every so often she wore big black, clunky Doc Martens. Sometimes Luke swung her up into the air and behind him, like they were jitterbugging or they were in *West Side Story*, so that her legs in those Doc Martens wrapped around his waist and Luke gave her piggyback rides. Luke was tall and blond, really big. He was good-looking like a guy on TV might be. He had that kind of jaw, the good-looking-guy jaw. He seemed older; maybe he *was* older. Henry said he'd gone to some fancy school for dyslexic kids up in Westchester before he transferred to Wildwood and they held him back a year. Since he was probably older to begin with—everyone at Wildwood was older, the boys were all older, kids at private school were intrinsically older—this made Luke *really* old, which probably accounted for the fact that he had strawberry blond stubble on his face most of the time, and once in a while he must have had to shave.

Luke wore T-shirts like everyone else at school, and flannel shirts in winter, but you could kind of imagine him in a suit someday, with short hair—his hair was long now, just past his ears, longer than Audrey's. You could kind of imagine him as a suit guy being an asshole. Audrey was slender, and not too tall. Jake didn't like to think about them being together much; Luke was so big, almost anything Jake could imagine them doing, even a hug or a friendly wrestle, involved Luke crushing her.

At night, the Manhattanites from the hill schools hung out in Manhattan on Park Avenue. All the kids from all the other schools—the city schools, East Side and West, the private school kids, the public school kids, the Hunter kids—they'd walk up and down Park Avenue, forming and reforming into groups, smoking and laughing too loud, looking for something to do. They were too young for the good stuff, still. Soon. Soon there would be clubs and music and bars, and even now there could be movies, but instead, they hung out on Park Avenue. Jake had just started hanging out at night, with his cell phone on vibrate in his front pocket; it was the only way his mom would let him go out. Riverdale was a whole new story; she hadn't wanted him on the subways alone or on the West Side Highway with some driver she hadn't met; she had to *know* the mom, she said—until last week, on his half birthday. Then she was forced by her own sense of fairness (Jake's mom was fair, he'd give her that) to let him be truly free. When he was in Manhattan, he'd take the bus across the park with Henry and Henry's twin, James, guys who lived in his hood—his mom liked him to travel in groups—and the three of them would meet up with McHenry, Davis, and Django. They were a crew. Henry had brought Jake in. The first week of school, Henry gave Jake the once-over and said, "You look cool," which saved him so much social misery; it was such an awesome thing for Henry to do, to size him up like that and bring him in, Jake figured he owed Henry his left nut or sympathetic karma for life. Maybe even money.

Sometimes Henry and James and Jake walked across the park at night, smoking cigarettes, and then they'd meet McHenry there, in the middle. He had this thing about this one particular park bench at the Big Circle. There was a plaque on it for his dead grandfather, the one who had made "all the money the rest of us live off of" in banking or something, and McHenry liked to sit on that bench and blow a joint. Every single time he fired one up and sucked the smoke in, he'd say in a strangled breath, "This one's for you, Pops," before passing the joint to James. Jake and Henry didn't smoke pot. They liked to play ball. Basketball. Henry liked to board. Ultimate Frisbee. That kind of stuff. They smoked cigarettes, once in a while. They weren't addicted or anything. They just sort of enjoyed it. It was cool in the park at night. At night the park felt a little bit menacing in a way that made Jake feel powerful just for being there. Like the sight of the four of them hanging out together was scary to someone else.

On Park Avenue, they'd stand around on the sidewalks in groups. Sometimes they'd head to a party. Other times, if no one was home at someone's apartment, all the kids would go there and they'd drink and listen to music and play video games and some of the kids would hook up. He was always in strangers' apartments, Jake. He was a new kid, so most of them were strange to him anyway, but a lot of the kids invited a lot of kids to these parties.

That's how you ended up making friends outside your school. People said, "Eli's folks are in Nantucket. Wanna come?" People said, "There's this Trinity dude whose parents said we could hang out on their terrace," and then a whole bunch of them would head over to the address someone shouted out and whatever doorman would let them up. Some of the apartments where these ad hoc parties were held were awesome—most were, really, because they were hanging on Park Avenue on the East Side—but some were small, too, like when there'd been a divorce, or a single mother and the kid was adopted or sperm-banked or whatever. Lesbians. Even on the East Side, lesbian parents tended to have smaller apartments.

All this easy come and go between kids who didn't know each other made the city feel small, and Jake liked that; he came from a small town and it made him feel comfortable. It also probably helped with hookups, because it was always easier to hook up with someone you didn't have to see the next day at school or the day after that and whom you could cross Park Avenue to avoid if you had to—Park Avenue had two lanes with convenient little islands in the middle, these natural barriers if you needed a bulwark of protection.

When they didn't go up to someone's apartment, they used the steps of the museum to smoke pot or drink beers. If they didn't smoke pot or drink, they stayed on Park Avenue. Mostly they walked around, calling out to one another, "S'up. S'up." It was rhetorical, not ever a question. Nothing was up, usually, unless something was. They were kids; they were terminally looking for something to do.

Audrey was never on Park Avenue. She lived in Riverdale, near school. So did Luke. Jake could only imagine what they did together in the woods by Luke's house or in his basement. He didn't like to think about it.

The kids who lived in Riverdale or nearby, in Cedar Knolls or Bronxville, if they had cars, if they had learner's permits, or if they had cool parents, they hung out at each other's houses, or in the woods near school. Some of them rode bikes, like he used to do at home. Audrey didn't look like the kind of girl who rode bikes. She wore those little gold ballet slippers to school and black jeans so narrow and straight they looked like tights. She was so hip, Audrey. She had such small ankles. She wore black eyeliner that matched her black eyes and that short swing of black hair, that slash that curled under her ear. How did she get so stylish? She was adopted. Was she found wrapped in a newspaper, like

his sister was, in the doorway to some orphanage? Did she just
have hip genes in her DNA? Was there some *something* that made
her cool here in Riverdale and that would have made her cool,
too, back in China? Or only here? How did she know to wear
those straight, narrow black jeans and those gold ballet slippers?
The little golden band of her skin, those ankles! Like bracelets
between pants and shoes. The Doc Martens in winter? With
those skinny long legs, the Doc Martens made her look like she
wore space boots.

Audrey's wrists looked like a sparrow's rib cage; that's what
always flashed through Jake's mind when he saw Luke grab her in
the hall, encircling her little wrist with his great big paw of a hand.
Ouch, you'll break the little bird's little rib cage. That's what he
thought, as Luke grabbed and pulled her along through the halls.
They were one of their grade's only couples, so the waters parted.
They were kind of special. Like a king and a high priestess. Soaring above the rest because they alone had found love.

"Wish I could get me one of those," McHenry once said,
when the couple walked past them. Jake had to squelch the urge
to punch McHenry in the gut; sometimes the dude was such an
asshole. Because McHenry said it like he knew that they had sex,
and he didn't know; none of them knew if Audrey and Luke had
sex, and Jake didn't like to think about it. Probably all the guys
felt that way, maybe, Jake thought, when they saw Audrey with
Luke, even possibly the gay ones, because in some weird way she
kind of looked like a pretty boy. Her chest was so flat. Just two
pushpin-size nipples poking through her black T-shirts, maybe
a little swell behind them, the puffy thickness of a bottom lip
after you kissed it. Jake had kissed girls—he'd hooked up—and

when you pulled away, even after only about fifteen minutes, their lips kind of inflated a little; there was no other word for it; they puffed. Once Jake stood behind Audrey at the water fountain and he saw the inside of that wrist when she turned the fountain on—the fountain was from the prehistoric age: you had to flip a metal lever like in a pinball machine for the water to come out—so he got to see the inside of her wrist and first he thought it was a tattoo and then he realized that what he was seeing were blue veins riding the tiny bones of that little wrist, like long worms you could see through her translucent skin. He wanted to gently press one. Would it melt under the flesh or would it rise to his touch? Jake doubted that Audrey ever ate anything. She looked like she lived on air.

Chinois.

It sounded like a fancy name for a fragrant, lacey breeze . . . or was that the word *Chinook*? He'd have to look it up.

So when Henry and James and McHenry and Django told him about this party Friday night up in Fieldston, in one of the Olivias' basements or pool house or whatever, Jake thought, sure, he'd go along. Maybe Audrey would be there and he'd see her eat something. That was kind of like his only impetus. Besides, the guys made him go. His mom and his sister were at some dumb sleepover anyway, and his dad worked a lot. It would be better than hanging out alone at home.

They stayed up in Riverdale when school let out. Davis and this kid Jonas joined them. They went over to Johnson Avenue and ate pizza. There was a lot of time to kill. They went to a nearby deli and bought some tallboys; McHenry's fake ID was on hand, even though nobody bothered to ask. They busted out of the deli as a laughing, raucous gang—like a multiheaded animal— and then they laughed even harder when they startled a group of older Orthodox men in payas talking on the sidewalk. There were a lot of Orthodox Jews in Riverdale. Jake was a Jew; that is, his mom was, so he was one, too, by Jewish *law*, she said, but he'd never met any Orthodox Jews or even seen this kind before they moved to New York. He kind of liked how they looked different, how they carried their inner beliefs on their backs. There was courage in that.

As a group, Jake and his friends practically owned the street. They jostled each other, taking up the whole sidewalk, laughing and smoking and making their way away from the strip of stores and into the residential neighborhood, the redbrick apartment buildings and then the "houses" houses, like a normal place. People had to step out of their way. Sometimes Jake took a step backward to let an old lady pass. Sometimes he didn't.

In the woods behind Jonas's house, McHenry fired up a joint and they stared out over the Hudson. Jake liked to look at the river; he liked the idea that the city ended, that there was water and another side. His mom said they would have a view of the river in their new apartment, and Jake was kind of looking forward to that, to being able to look out his window and see the water move. Jake and Henry smoked cigarettes and drank beers, James and Django, too. Davis smoked with McHenry and didn't want a beer; he said the beer would interfere with his buzz. There were boats on the Hudson, long industrial-looking barges and sleek motor craft, one old-fashioned sailboat with multiple sails, swelling in the breeze like flags, which looked like a pirate ship. "Ahoy there, mateys," said McHenry, like he was being funny and this was some hilarious take on some original vision thing that he alone possessed. The guy was a total asshole. Jake had no idea why they all hung out with him, but Jake was too new, and ultimately too nice—he hated that he was so nice—to say or do much about it. Then they all needed to pee, so they did, on a stand of trees. McHenry and Davis had a sword fight until Henry said, "Jesus, you guys are puerile," and then they turned around and tried to pee on Henry, somebody's stream hitting the bottom of Henry's jeans in a little arc of stitching, which really pissed him off. Jake noticed then that McHenry wasn't circumcised and it was the first time he'd ever seen one up close.

"What are you staring at, faggot?" said McHenry. He actually looked steamed.

"Aw, he's never seen a dog in a bun before," said Henry, getting it. "I can't believe you pissed on my fucking pants."

They had a lot of time to kill, and it was showing. There were rips in the fragile membrane encasing their camaraderie. They could easily get into a fight or something. They were all coming down a little now, and the evening hadn't even begun yet. Even the horizon was still light, though the water was getting darker, as if night started from the river and bled its way up toward the sky.

"Come on, let's just go to Jonas's house and play Xbox," said Davis. Ever the paxmeister, the peacemaker, another nice guy.

Jonas shrugged. "All right with me." So they spent a couple of hours like that in Jonas's basement, playing Xbox, watching TV, until their brains fried. Jake kind of wished he still lived in Ithaca right then. He kind of wished he were right that minute back in

Ithaca, on Buffalo Street, going down the hill on his bike. Buffalo Street was so steep you had to be nuts to go down it without your hand brakes on, but Jake liked to; he even liked to close his eyes, which was kind of close to committing suicide, it was such a nuts thing to do. He liked the way the wind felt rushing through his hair, drying off the sweat on his scalp, on his neck, in his armpits, as it flew up his shirtsleeves, billowing out his back like a sail. He liked flying blind.

Jonas's mom was going out for the night, but she ordered in Chinese food for them first. "You boys can have whatever you want," she said. "Jo, there's money in the money jar." So they ate spare ribs and egg rolls standing up, screaming at each other over the Xbox. They ate noodles straight out of the cartons, with their splintery wooden chopsticks, no one thinking to grab a plate. It was a good, boring time, until the hours passed and they were ready to go to the party, where there were girls and things could possibly change.

So they walked up the hill en masse to Olivia's, running into Arthur Gladstone and his band of freaks on the way. Arthur was old-school punk: dog collar, Sex Pistols T-shirt, boots with chains. It was sort of funny, Jake thought, how there was always a small group of hippies and punks, greasers, too, wherever you went to school. Like once the stuff got in the water it was inevitable that a few kids would be born every year beamed up from another era. In Ithaca there was a guy who'd tattooed every inch of his body, including his entire face. And he was a dad! Jake had seen him pushing a stroller on the Commons, his baby's cheeks as fresh and white as a pork bun. Did the kid puzzle over all his father's ink? Or did he just figure, that's my dad? Maybe Jake's own offspring would be obsessed with ancient Xbox games and would spend their time sitting around arguing about them, which ones rocked and which ones sucked, the way his dad and his college friends would sit around fighting about Bob Dylan albums. Some of Arthur's posse didn't even go to Wildwood—they went to Kennedy, the local public high school, and two of those dudes wore Mohawks. Jake's six-year-old baby sister wore dog collars and even she knew she was wearing them as a joke.

"Coco has an instinctive, irreverent, jocose flair for the burlesque," Henry once said, solemnly. "Someday I shall marry her."

Dream on, Jake had thought. But he said nothing.

"It's not happening," said Arthur, in dint of a greeting.

"What?" said McHenry. "What's not happening, you fascist fuck?"

"Olivia's parents decided to go to the country and to bring Olivia, so they can all eat family dinner." Arthur sneered and spat on the sidewalk. "She's failing math again." He was wearing purple eye shadow, and for a minute Jake expected the spit to come out pink and blue, but it didn't.

"Bummer," said McHenry. He turned to his boys. "Now what?"

There wasn't much else to do if there was no party. Jake mentally consulted the express bus schedule. He was a twenty-minute walk from the closest stop.

"Daisy Cavanaugh said we could all come to her place. Her folks are in Cyprus avoiding taxes," said Arthur.

"Daisy Cavanaugh is in eighth grade," said McHenry in disgust. "She's a middle school pig and a slut," he added.

Jake didn't know Daisy Cavanaugh. He lifted an eyebrow at Henry.

Henry shrugged, his skateboarder's hair touching his shoulders as they rose. "Aww, she's all right," he said to McHenry. "She's got a nice house," he said to Jake.

"McMansion," said Arthur. "Fucking movie theater in the basement, backyard pool. Her father is heir to some label fortune."

"Label fortune?" said Jake.

"You know, like Calvin Klein? The labels?" said Arthur.

Davis said, "We've got nothing better to do. We've got nowhere else to go."

"Ain't that the truth," said McHenry. He and Davis high-fived.

They followed Arthur and his freak squad to the Cavanaughs'.

Daisy Cavanaugh's house was one of the biggest houses in Riverdale. It was white, modern; each of its three glassy levels seemed to rise out at some new angle to better capture a view of the Hudson. It was almost as if someone had moved the house east from California, it had so little in common with the surrounding Tudors and neo-Georgians. The place was an advertisement for itself.

It wasn't that steep a climb up the road, but McHenry kept pounding his chest and coughing. As he went, he kept saying, "Got to lay off the stogies," which Jake took as an affectation, although maybe it wasn't; maybe, at seventeen, McHenry had already totaled his lungs. They could hear music, really loud music, rocking out, and the blue light of the first level of the house glowed like there was a swimming pool inside of it, even though everyone said the swimming pool was out back. The party was downstairs. The main entrance to the house was farther up the road. This bottom tier was where the garage was, the little movie theater Arthur had mentioned, the playroom, and the wet bar. The sauna. The changing room that led out to the pool. Henry explained all of this to Jake. He'd been there once, Henry said, when the Cavanaughs threw a retirement party for some kindergarten teacher that he and Daisy had suffered through during different years, and all her ex-pupils and their families had been invited to send her off.

McHenry went in first and scoped the place, while the boys huddled together on the road, Arthur passing around a joint. It was getting cold outside, even though it was May. The wind was whipping across the river, and Jake half wished he was home, watching a movie. Arthur and his friends weren't exactly mesmerizing conversationalists, and the rest of the guys had all pretty much run out of shit to say. So they stood, hands in pockets, shifting their weight, eyeing each other, bouncing on their toes. Davis was on his cell phone texting around, looking for other action, in case this party was officially over.

"Maya and Chloe are at Chloe's highlighting their hair. Cantor and a bunch of dudes are in the East Village at the Blue and Gold, but how the hell would we get there? Josh says there's a crew hanging on Park Avenue. Been there." And then, turning to Django: "I dunno. Maybe we should have stayed in town." He was fast on that thing.

"So let's go back," said Django, who was kind of nerdy and hardly talked, unless he was talking to Davis. "I'm down with that."

Jake had turned to Henry and whispered, "I think I'm going to head home," when a Lexus sedan pulled up behind them. Luke, the fucker, was driving. Audrey was sitting outside on the windowsill of the passenger seat, her butt resting in the tight little hammock of her black jeans, beating a drumbeat on the roof of the car with her fists. "Aloha, boys," she said, as Luke, grinning, pulled past them and into the driveway.

McHenry came outside then with a thumb up. "There's beers inside," he said. When he passed Luke, who was getting out of the car, they bumped fists (they hung out sometimes, a fact that upped McHenry's ante, which he was well aware of), and then Luke went around to Audrey's side and sort of swung her out of the window. She wrapped her arms and legs around him, clinging like a koala cub, and he carried her into the house.

Henry looked at Jake looking at Audrey.

"Not in this lifetime," said Henry.

"Shut up," said Jake.

There was a moment between them; there had never been a moment between them before.

Then Henry said, "C'mon man, the dude says there's beers inside." He kind of patted Jake on his shoulder and then they followed the rest of the guys, who were already trailing after McHenry into the house.

Inside, the foyer was large and white with a double-height ceiling, and Jake could see big pieces of art hanging in the living room, which was off to the right. He could see bright copper walls in the dining room, which was off to the left. There was a long, gracious staircase heading up to the bedrooms.

"Downstairs," said Henry, gently now, leading him.

McHenry had already disappeared down the stairs. The floors were pickled white. How did they keep this house so bright and clean? Jake wondered, feeling like his mother's son, hating himself for wondering. He followed Arthur. Then Davis and Jonas and Django followed him, and Henry and James brought up the rear, the two of them twinning the way they sometimes did, heads together, leaving everyone out, probably talking about him, Jake thought, and then killed the thought because it was stupid and would get him nowhere. As they went down the stairs, they passed a couple of couples heading up to the bedrooms: newbie couples, hooking up. Jake wanted to call ahead, to ask McHenry if he'd seen Audrey, if he'd seen her and Luke go up those stairs, but he knew better than to open himself to shit like that.

Downstairs was like something out of a movie. One of those eighties flicks that he and Henry liked to watch ironically: *Pretty in Pink* or that *Some Kind of Wonderful* he'd been forced to sit through at a girl's party back in Ithaca. It all just smelled of money; there was like a whole entertainment complex downstairs. There was an amazing music system, Live Snake was blaring, and the furniture looked too expensive and mod to sit on, all leather and chrome, with shaggy white throw rugs, but there were bowls of chips and salsa and M&Ms on the metal-and-glass coffee tables like at any party anywhere, cans of Coke. Arthur and his crowd peeled off toward the pool table, but McHenry motioned his crew to follow him down the hallway. There were beers in the Japanese bathtub off the sauna—he'd told them this outside—and it was true, their green necks studding the ice like emeralds. Each boy grabbed a bottle. The glass felt cool and smooth between Jake's thumb and forefinger, resting in the webbing.

A bunch of kids from school were sitting on leather couches, and through an open door Jake could see the private screening room. There were some couples making out in there, and a few boys whose names he didn't know yelling at the screen. *Scarface.* Al Pacino had just fallen face-first into a pile of cocaine, and the dudes were cheering.

"Hey, Daisy," said Henry. "Thanks for moving the party here."

Jake turned around and met their hostess. She was a short, plump, prettyish girl with a baby face, too-tight jeans tucked into her UGGs. Her blond hair was bleached white and hanging loose, some of the layers pushed behind her ears, which hosted a lot of earrings, hoops scaling the rim. She looked like an eleven year-old with too much makeup on. Raccoon eyes, but bright blue. Little breasts, a black lace bra visible through her tank top. She would be prettier, he thought, if she washed off all that goo.

"Hey, Henry," she said. "Hey, Jake."

He was surprised Daisy knew his name. He didn't remember seeing her around school.

"Either of you guys want a friendship bracelet?" She held out a palm full of red strings with beads on them.

"Sure," said Henry, and she tied one around his wrist. "Make that a double, for my friend here." Henry gestured with his head toward Jake, who obediently held out his arm.

Daisy smiled up at him as she tied the bracelet on.

"There's beer," she said, in a way that made Jake wince. It was so eager. He tipped his bottle her way and said, "Thanks. We already partook." Then he telescoped his neck, looking up and past Daisy. He didn't see Audrey anywhere. His eyes locked with Henry's, who shook his head.

"Fuck you," said Jake.

"What's your problem, man?" said Henry. His face was turning red. "I'm just looking out for you. Sheesh, ma-meesh." He turned away and headed toward the movie.

Jake took another swig of his beer, almost emptying it.

"Do you want another beer, Jake? I can get you one," said Daisy. She was smiling up at him.

All of a sudden, Jake felt a rising swell of anger. Fuck Henry. Fuck Audrey. So what if she was upstairs sucking Luke off? He didn't give a flying fuck.

"That would be great, Daisy," he said. "I mean, I can get it myself . . ."

"We can go get it together," she said. She gave his hand a little squeeze. Jake looked down at her hand in surprise—he didn't expect to find it there. Her fingernail polish was chipped and the nail beds themselves still looked square, like a kid's. For a moment he wondered, at what age do a girl's fingernails elongate? Was it a puberty thing? Or did it come after, the way beards sometimes did? Coco's nails looked like this, like little old-fashioned TV sets, tiny boxes. Daisy's hand even felt like a baby's. Like a baby bear, he inexplicably thought; he even said this to himself, in his mind, "Her hand feels like a little paw, a teddy bear's paw." He was so weird; he couldn't stand himself sometimes.

What the fuck. Jake squeezed her hand back. Daisy smiled at him, a big, wide smile, as if the squeeze had fortified her, like it was an extrasensory protein drink. Her reaction alone made him swagger. He started to get hard. She gently tugged on his hand and led him through the throngs of people and toward the tub. He might as well get drunk, he thought. It was a party.

They were making out in the back of the screening room, Jake sitting in an aisle seat, Daisy in his lap, her feet not quite grazing the floor. He had one hand up her tank top, on top of her bra, which was lacey and scratchy. Her whole breast fit inside the circumference of his palm, like a rubber ball. The film was long over, but the screen still displayed light. They weren't the only couple in there. There were three others, all bathed in that bluish movie afterglow. Jake periodically counted his companions whenever he came up for air or to wipe his mouth. For some reason, he didn't want to be alone with Daisy. It was like they kept him from going too far. He was hard, and Daisy kept shifting in his lap. She had her arms around his neck and every so often she would stroke his back and shoulders.

"Mmmm," she said. "You feel so good. Your muscles are so big," she whispered into his ear, her tongue flicking around the rim, hot and wet.

Jake had drunk a lot and felt dizzy. He did not have big muscles. So it sort of grossed him out when she said that. Plus, he was feeling kind of sick. Like maybe, eventually, before the night was over, he might throw up.

"Jacobyyy," McHenry said, in a funny, fratty voice. "Jacobyyy and fucking Meyers . . ."

Jake looked up past Daisy's blond head, his lips still locked on hers. There were Luke and McHenry, laughing at him.

Luke said, "Hey, dude, robbing the cradle?" Audrey stood a little behind Luke, but he put his arm around her waist and swung her around in front like a protective shield or a hostage in a standoff. He looked a little trashed, Luke. He was a little wild with her, and her feet flew off the floor before they landed.

"Whee," Audrey deadpanned, rolling her eyes.

"Come on," said Daisy, looking up at them, her expression eager. "They're out of my room now. Jake, we can go upstairs . . ."

Jake looked at her baby face. It was like a bright, round moon, glowing and open. He looked at Luke and at Audrey and at McHenry.

"Naw, Daisy," he said. "It's late. I better be getting home . . ."

"What's your hurry, dude," said McHenry. "Give the lady what she wants."

Jake stood up, spilling Daisy out of his lap.

Audrey caught Daisy's left arm as she staggered.

"Whoa," said Audrey.

"Jake," said Daisy.

"Sorry, Daisy," said Jake, actually feeling sorry. "I shouldn't have done that. I shouldn't have done any of that. I'm drunk, I guess. I got up too fast. Are you all right? God, I'm sorry."

"I'm fine," said Daisy, turning pink. "Why are you talking like that?"

"I'm drunk." He looked around. "Where's Henry?" he said over her shoulder to McHenry.

"I think he left," said McHenry.

"He left?"

Jake couldn't believe that Henry would leave without him.

"I think he got a ride with somebody, or they split a Miles taxi. I don't know, he bounced."

"James?"

"What do you think," said McHenry. He shook his head, like Jake was a moron. "They're twins, man."

"So you missed your ride," said Daisy, giving Jake's hand a tug. "Let's go upstairs. My parents are away till tomorrow afternoon. You could sleep over."

"A regular sleepover date," said Luke. "Buddy, go for it." He looked pretty drunk to Jake, a lot drunker than Jake was. Luke kind of slurred his words when he talked. Maybe he was on something?

Audrey looked at Luke with cool eyes. You couldn't tell what she was thinking. That he was an asshole or that this was a funny joke; either one, or something different. Audrey didn't say anything. Maybe she didn't think anything. Maybe what Jake took for mystery was vacancy; a big blank banner of stretched nothing. Or maybe it was a bandage for inner torment, plastic and gummy, wrapping her up. Maybe she ached inside like he did. She was an enigma. An oracle. A sphinx.

"She looks like jailbait to me, man," said McHenry, looking at Daisy. "But then again, you're not old enough yourself, are you? Luke's right, go for it. I mean if you're both statutory, what the fuck?" He shrugged.

McHenry looked to Luke for approval. The look was too needy to be cool, but Luke seemed too fucked up to notice. He nodded at McHenry with an endorsing grin. That fucking jaw.

He could get all the chicks in the world with a jaw like that. No matter how sloppy drunk Luke was, there was no denying his beauty. Luke got better looking, it seemed, the more fucked up he was, with his pink cheeks and glowing blue eyes, his blond hair and red-and-yellow stubble.

Audrey peeled Luke's arms away from around her waist. Once released, one of his giant hands went below his nose and he sniffed hard. A little thread of clear mucus clung to his knuckles in the moment it took to brush it away. Maybe they were all on coke.

"Daisy," said Audrey, standing up and stretching. Her black T-shirt lifted up with her arms and Jake could see she had a little gold ring piercing her navel. God, he hated her. It was as if she'd pierced her navel just to get at him. "I have to pee. Wanna come with?" she said.

So she was human after all: she had to pee. Hot, golden pee came sluicing out of her. He thought about getting down on his knees and catching it in a cup made of his hands. And she could be nice. Nice to Daisy. Nicer than Jake was.

He loved her again. Suddenly he loved Audrey with all his heart. He would do anything just to touch her. To smell her skin.

"Yeah, go pee with Audrey," said Luke, trying to suppress his glee. "I love peeing with Audrey. Sometimes she holds my thing . . ."

"You're an asshole," said Audrey.

He pulled his arms around her again and tightened his grip around her chest and waist and started to smother her neck in kisses.

"But I'm your asshole," said Luke.

Audrey tried to squirm out of his grasp, but then she giggled, and he caught her chin with one hand and turned her face to his for a long, too-long, movie star kiss.

They were putting on a show. This much was clear. For his benefit. To torture him.

"Come on, Jake," said Daisy, tugging at him.

"No," said Jake.

"Come on, Jakey," said Daisy, and she tried to kiss him on the neck, mimicking Luke.

"No, I said, no," said Jake, pushing her aside. He pushed her so hard she flew against McHenry. "Leave me alone," Jake said.

"Hey," said McHenry, his hands flying up as if he were under arrest, as if he were saying, "I didn't do it."

"Jake!" said Audrey, in an admonishing tone, as Daisy began to cry.

"I'm sorry, Daisy," said Jake, reaching out, petting the air, then pulling his hand back to his side. "Goddamn it, I'm sorry. You're just way too young." He blurted this out.

"I am not," Daisy said through her tears, mascara running down her face. She looked and sounded ridiculous.

Jake looked at her smeared mouth. He was the one who'd smeared it.

"I am not," she said again, and she stamped her foot.

McHenry snorted and stamped his foot, and then everybody laughed. Everybody including Jake, including Audrey. Daisy's face went bright red.

"I gotta get out of here," said Jake. He pushed his way through the party.

"C'mon, we can share a cab," McHenry called after him. But Jake didn't stop. He didn't stop until he'd climbed the stairs and walked out of the house and into the fresh, cool air. You could smell the trees out there.

Outside, it was as if they lived in a real place, with houses and lawns, a place he could recognize. He climbed up the hill and walked to the highway. He didn't stop walking. He walked and walked, all the way down the sidewalk that hemmed the highway and then down the hill and into Kingsbridge and then down, down, down the stairs into the subway. He waited on the platform and then he got on the subway and he took it home.

By the time Jake got back to the apartment, it was late. Way late. Way later than he'd ever been up or out before. The streets outside were quiet. He was lucky his mom wasn't there to call the cops or something. His dad was already asleep. That was the good thing about his dad. He cared, but he didn't. Jake knocked on his father's door and his dad grunted and Jake said, "I'm home," like he was trained to do, and his dad said, "I'm glad, son."

It was the *son* that made Jake weep. He lay on his bed and for a while he cried into his pillow. It was so fucked up. He felt all tangled and put out, like he didn't know himself anymore and he couldn't think of anyone on the planet who did. He didn't belong here, in the city, in this apartment, at this school, or in this family, and he didn't belong back in Ithaca anymore, either—he'd gone back over spring break and that had been kind of fun but kind of weak and pathetic, too; everyone was a little too nice to him, like he was a foreigner or a cripple. He'd hooked up in Ithaca, but not with a thirteen-year-old, with a sixteen-year-old, Johanna

Shoenstein, a normal girl who was older. Not like that baby he'd been with tonight. Jake felt a hot wave of embarrassment and shame just thinking about Daisy, about his hand on her breast, on the outside of her bra—he was such an idiot! He thought about Luke and McHenry and Audrey laughing at him, and when he thought about her he shoved his head into the pillow until it felt like he couldn't breathe. Then the pillow got wet, it got soggy, and when he pulled away, strings of drool clung to the pillow and the corner of his mouth, which was disgusting. Jake turned the pillow over and pounded it with his fist, and put the back of his head down on the fresh side. He thought about Daisy again and he cringed. His gut shriveled up into his chest. It pushed his lungs up and into his throat. It was hard to breathe, he felt so ashamed of himself. He should never have hooked up with her. But he'd said no. That was the right thing to do, right? She was too young, and he was a virgin anyway. He didn't want to do it with Daisy. Maybe he should have done it, maybe it would have been cool to have done it and gotten it out of the way—Henry was always talking about that, getting it done and out of the way. Henry had gotten his out of the way on a spring break ski trip with his youth group this year, while Jake was innocently making out with Johanna in Ithaca like some dumb middle-schooler, but who was there to verify that? Just because Henry said so? The girl in the story didn't even have a name. James wouldn't validate either way. Daisy had been begging for it. It wasn't taking advantage; if a girl wanted to hook up—his mom was always saying don't take advantage of a girl, but what if a girl wanted to be taken advantage of? His mom was like stuck back in the seventies, all her crap about feminism and the way girls dressed these days . . .

but what if the girl wants the hookup? If she begs for it? Did his
mom ever think about that?

It never would have occurred to him to hook up with Daisy if
she hadn't thrown herself at him. All that beer. Fucking Audrey.

He thought about Audrey, that golden ring on her golden belly.
His hand instinctively unzipped his jeans. His hand went down
to it, and it unleashed, hard and smooth, rising up to meet his
hand. Maybe Audrey thought he was a good guy for saying no to
Daisy. Maybe Audrey thought he was a sleaze and a dweeb. He'd
pushed Daisy; he'd pushed Daisy off of him. Audrey couldn't have
liked that. Nobody would like that, a guy pushing a girl. God, he
was an idiot. He tried to remember Audrey's face in that horrible
moment when his hands, not Jake, but Jake's hands alone, had
pushed Daisy, but he couldn't remember; he couldn't remember
the look on Audrey's face. His left fist was going faster and faster
now. It tightened, and even though his skin was too dry and the
fist was burning, right now he liked it that way and he didn't stop
to spit or go for the Aveeno lotion. Maybe Audrey liked that he'd
been rough with Daisy. Who knew? She liked Luke. And Luke
was a jerk. Luke was always swinging her around. Maybe Audrey
liked it nasty.

Jake came in loud, angry spurts, and then there was jizz all
over his bed, which was disgusting. He took his T-shirt off and
rubbed the jizz off on the shirt and then he stripped the sheets
and put the whole mess plus his boxers into his hamper, wondering how he was going to explain all this laundry to his mom.

He got up and went to his closet to get some clean sheets
and remade the bed. He put on a new T-shirt, fresh underwear,
pajama pants. He was too wired to go to sleep. So he turned on

the computer and checked his email. There was a missive from
Henry: "sry we split w/out u, but yr hands wr full . . ." Jake tried
to decipher the tone. Conciliatory? Or was Henry also making
fun of him? Jake chose conciliatory, because he needed him. He
wrote back: "Drunk. Don't ever let me do that again." Then he
closed his laptop and climbed into bed. And then he got up and
out of it. He went back to his computer. Googled "Ithaca, New
York." Shut the laptop again and went back to bed. He could read
old Spider-Man comics. That's what he could do, and he did. He
read them till he fell asleep finally, and then he heard his mother
and sister coming in the front door.

"Did you have a good time last night?" Jake's mom asked as Jake
opened the refrigerator.

She looked awful. Her brown eyes were red, and her skin
was gray and translucent—he could see her veins throbbing in
her temples. She looked a little old, a little like she would probably look like as an old lady, her hair twisted up in a bun that
way, her T-shirt all sweaty and wrinkled. His mom looked the
way she looked after one of them had been up all night with the
throw-up flu and she'd been holding their heads, aiming them
over the toilet, wiping their mouths. She looked a little like his
grandma had looked before she died. Jake did not like looking
at her right now.

So he scanned the interior of the refrigerator. Was there Sunny
D inside? Milk? Something he'd want to down first thing in the
morning? His mom hated it when he drank coffee. Said it might
stunt his growth, when nothing seemed to stop him; his arms and

legs already felt too long for his body, but whatever. He drank coffee every day at school, hoping to be normal.

"Yeah, I guess so," he said, finally answering her question. "I guess I had a good time, yeah."

He lifted out a gallon of milk and brought it to his lips. He took a long slug and put the container back inside. He turned to her, hoping what, that he could talk to her? That she would rescue him?

She turned off the stove. The teakettle hadn't even boiled yet. How could he tell her about hooking up with Daisy? Giving her that shove? Drinking too much? His mom was always going on and on about how grateful blah blah she was that she could trust him.

He was hoping she could magically intuit all of this, hoping that she could read his mind and instantly forgive him, like she used to; she could read his mind and forgive him all in an instant when he was young. Instead, she said, "All right, then, Mom's got a hangover," and sidled past him, almost like she wasn't his mom, almost like she was a roommate or a grown-up stranger who lived in his apartment. As if she really didn't know or care if there was anything wrong with him or not.

"Way to go, Mom," Jake said.

She shuffled off to her room to sleep it off.

It was already there. By noon, she'd already shot the damn thing and sent it to him. Daisymae@yahoo.com. The email was in Jake's in-box. He downloaded it and couldn't believe what he saw; Jake had never seen anything like it before—even at McHenry's, even when they were at McHenry's and McHenry Googled stuff like "Big Booty" and "Two Girls One Cup" and they all gathered around until they got bored. But this was not boring. Jake was the opposite of bored. Right now, Jake couldn't believe what he actually was watching. Was he supposed to be watching this? Was it legal?

He turned the computer off. He turned the computer off just by pressing the button. He didn't hit the Apple and cursor down or any of the stuff that he always did every day by rote. He just shut it down. You could lose data that way, but he wasn't thinking at the moment. He just did it. It was what his science teacher would have called an autonomic response.

He waited a minute and breathed hard. There was sweat running down the back of his T-shirt. Then he pressed the button and turned the computer back on.

Then he had to wait, he had to wait so long, he couldn't believe he had to wait so long. He should never have turned the computer off! Now he had to wait first for the black-and-white pinwheel to whirl around and then the rainbow-colored one—which he despised. And then he realized he'd already downloaded the thing. He didn't need to log on. So he just double-clicked and he watched it again. Daisy in that skirt. Daisy with that music. Daisy with no underwear. Daisy.

Was this pornography? Was it even sexy? He thought it was sexy, but he wasn't sure. He felt hard and he felt soft. It was like a hot potato. He had to fling it to someone else.

"Check it out," he typed. Then he forwarded the email on to Henry.

He watched the video again. He watched it over and over.

His phone began to vibrate. It made a horrible sound as it buzzed against the floor in the pocket of his jeans, where he'd left it. He looked up, and the jeans looked like they were shuddering, like they were ashamed and shuddering. Like they felt guilty about where they had been the night before. On his body. On his horrible, disgusting body. Jake reached out and pulled them over with his foot—there were hairs on his toes; when had he gotten hairs on his toes? He was so gross!—and then he leaned over and picked them up. By the time he'd worked the phone out of his pocket, the caller had gone to voice mail. He phoned in for his message. It was Henry.

"Jake, dude, what the fuck? Call me," said Henry.

So he did. He called Henry. He called him right back, but it was too late. In the thirty seconds it had taken him to retrieve and return the call, Henry had already forwarded the thing on to James and Davis. James was sitting in front of *his* laptop in the next room in their apartment. "Whoa, shit," he yelled. "C'mere."

"No, dude," Henry called out to him. "You come here."

Neither brother could stop watching.

By Monday, it was all over; all over school. Everyone had seen it during the weekend, and the ones who hadn't, they heard about it as soon as they touched down on campus. Kids were downloading it and watching it in the library. Henry had forwarded it to James and McHenry. James had instantly downloaded it, watched the thing, and once summoned, gotten up from his desk and walked into Henry's room while Henry was taking Jake's freaked-out call. By that time, McHenry had forwarded it on to Django and Davis, and then McHenry sent it to five or six other guys—only three from Wildwood, including Luke, and then two or three more from camp. And then forgot about it. It was all over the school and all over the city. Connecticut. Kids were finding it on porno sites. It was all over the country, maybe the world, even. So fast. Just like that. Forward and Send. It was kind of incredible how fast it went. Faster than fire. Practically the speed of sound or even light.

(By the end of the week, Jake was forwarded the video by a friend from Ithaca who didn't even know it had started in New York, even though it had made the news by then, even though there had been helicopters from Eyewitness News up at school, even though it had been in the *New York Post*.)

Daisy. "Daisy Up at Bat." That was the porno listing that Henry forwarded to Jake, Monday morning before they left for the subway, neither of them sleeping the night before, trying breathlessly to keep track. The fucking video was everywhere. It clogged up Jake's in-box; people sent it to him without knowing it was meant for him, that he was its inspiration and its muse, that he was its disseminator. It was just everywhere.

"Ubiquitous," said Henry on the subway. "Ecumenical. Panoramic. Catholic."

"Broadcast," said Jake, miserably. "*She* sent it to me," he said to Henry, for like the fifty-eight millionth time.

"Her choice," said Henry.

"She knew it was forwardable," said Jake.

"Yes, indeed," said Henry. "She probably wanted you to forward it. She was asking for it. You're innocent, dude. Don't worry about it."

When they hit campus, Jake kept his head down. Henry walked broad-shouldered beside him. Like a bodyguard. But it didn't take long, really. "Later, dude," said Henry, peeling out to go to Conceptual Math. It was all Jake could do to keep himself from running down the hall after him. He'd felt oddly protected, having Henry there. Jake had science first period, and when he slid into his seat just as the bell rang, Zack Bledsoe whispered into his ear, "Way to go, babe." Zack Bledsoe called him babe, which was weird in and of itself, and slightly nauseating. Jake spent the whole period internally freaking out; he didn't hear one thing Mr. Carmichael had to say about chemistry. When the bell rang, he blinked and looked around like he'd had a seizure or something, like he'd just woken up from a coma.

"Hey, Zack," Jake said, "do you think I could take a look at your notes?"

"Sure, babe," said Zack, "if you share your beauty secrets with me." Then he laughed way too loudly and his belly shook.

Jake had gym second period, which was great because he could shoot hoops and let off a little steam. But when he was changing in the locker room, Django came up to him and asked, "Did you tell Daisy to do that?" Which was weird, because Django never said very much, and why would Jake tell Daisy to do a thing like that?

"No," said Jake.

"My cousin in New Jersey saw it," said Django. "He sent me the link."

This made Jake feel a little bit sick. Like maybe he should go to the nurse and go home?

"I feel a little bit sick," said Jake to nobody. And nobody said anything.

After gym, Jake hurried over to the History Building without taking a shower. He had basketball practice after school, and days like today often he didn't even bother to change. He was still wearing his basketball shorts and school jersey when he entered the building. He saw his own reflection in the glass of the building door and he read the Wildwood Wildcats logo backward. So it *was* him residing in his body even if he felt like an imposter.

"Pond scum," whispered some girl Jake didn't know, right into his ear, as he held the door open for her. He almost jumped out of his skin. Does she mean me? he thought. He watched the girl walk down the hall, trying to figure out who she was . . . just another brown-haired girl in a ponytail, a tank top. How docs she know who I am? he thought.

A group of kids in the back of the classroom snickered when he entered.

"Yo, Casanova," this kid Eli called out. The girls giggled. Karenna Mercer said, "When are you going to make a video for Daisy? You know, the boy version . . ."

"Virgin or version?" said Eli. Everybody laughed.

Why? Jake thought. Was that a funny joke?

Then Ms. Hemphill and Ms. Schwartzman, his Deconstructing America co-teachers, entered the room. Ms. Schwartzman was so pregnant; sometimes you could see the baby kick beneath her shirt, like an alien, like it was trying to pop out. Now and again she said, "Oooh," when her shirtfront jumped, and some of the girls screamed.

"Settle down, everybody," said Ms. Hemphill. "Karenna, let's hear your oral presentation on the Alexis de Tocqueville essay

'Why the Americans Are So Restless in the Midst of Their Prosperity,' from *Democracy in America*."

Jake started to relax as Karenna gathered up her notes. He could zone through the whole period while she droned on, and then maybe go to the nurse's office after all. That's when the classroom door opened and the assistant head of the high school, Ms. Rodriguez, walked in.

"I'm here for Jacob Bergamot," she said, and for one bizarre moment, Jake wondered, did my dad have a heart attack? Because why else would the assistant head of school come calling? But of course that's not why; he knew that was not why, as he gathered up his stuff, his books and his backpack, and, still in his basketball uniform, followed Ms. Rodriguez and her clicking heels out of the classroom, the hot stares of his classmates focusing on him like eighteen laser beams, his heart beating wildly in his throat. It felt like the other kids could see right through his skin and into his churning gut. Kind of like the cow with the plastic window in its side that he'd seen every year at the Cornell Ag School fair growing up—an open display of its digestive system. Ms. Rodriguez had come because of Daisy, because of Daisy and her video. Everyone knew that. Everyone knew this moment was coming, except Jake, who'd been lying to himself. This much was clear, the sheer inevitability of his downfall, from the disgusted look on Ms. Rodriguez's face as she marched him out of the room, to the way everyone gaped at his disgrace like he had a porthole window in his side, like they could see his innards grinding into shit.

The Upper School librarian had caught sight of the video over some girl's shoulder on one of the school's PCs and that was that. Jake was pulled out of third-period history, and Henry and

McHenry and Davis and Django were pulled out of AP Chemistry and Advanced Math. By noon, Jake's mom was on her way to school, and he had already been suspended. His dad was in a very important meeting at work and could not be disturbed.

He learned all this in the head of school's office. Mr. Threadgill. Mr. Threadgill appeared to be enjoying himself as he told Jake how much trouble he was in before Jake's mom arrived, but Threadgill waited until his mom got there to view the video. Then it was Jake, his mom, and Threadgill, sitting together in Threadgill's office. The guy was balding but with a beard, a Van Dyke, as if he could make up for the lack of hair on his head with hair on his chin. It reminded Jake of pubic hair, of pubic hair on his face, under Threadgill's nose, which was small and quivering with repressed rage, and surrounding his lips, which were too red, like a monkey's anus. He was wearing a shirt and tie, but no jacket, as if it was too steamy in his office and he'd had to sling his tweed jacket over the back of his chair. Jake's mom was wearing a skirt and sweater set; he couldn't recall ever seeing her in that outfit before. Pink top, cream-colored bottom. She was dressed like a pretty suburban mom on TV.

"Jake!" she'd said when she arrived, like she'd just come upon him in a hospital emergency room, like he was on a stretcher, hooked up to some machine that beeped, although Jake was just sitting on a wooden bench outside Threadgill's office, waiting for her. Threadgill moved him into a conference room to wait by himself, while Threadgill filled her in, or threatened her, or threatened Jake—whatever Threadgill wanted. Jake waited on that bench forever. Through the window in the wooden conference room door, Jake saw Henry and his mom walk by.

And then, finally, Jake was called in by Threadgill's secretary, and when he walked back into the head of school's office, he saw that his mom had been crying. Her eyes were red and her nose was pink. She had a balled-up tissue in her fist and she kept dabbing at her nose, which was running. She did not look Jake in the eye when he walked in.

"Take a seat," said Threadgill, gesturing toward the empty chair leaning against the wall, across from his mother. Jake noticed that his left leg was jiggling.

Jake pulled the chair away from the wall and set it in line with his mom's.

"Jacob, I wanted your mother to see this with you in the room," said Threadgill. He said this with certainty, like he was certain he was doing the right thing. Then he swiveled his PC monitor around so that all three of them could see the screen and he scooted his own chair back. The computer looked a little like E.T., Jake thought, with its long black accordion neck and wide white monitor. (His dad had ordered *E.T.* on Netflix; Coco loved it, but Jake had found it too sad to watch and wandered away into his bedroom.) Then Threadgill, smug and plump and trying hard to look blank beneath his beard, hit the Play button.

And there it was: Daisy. The zits on her cheek. The earrings on her ear, that awful dyed hair. *I love to love you, baby.* Beyoncé. Jake knew what was coming next. Daisy and her sex dance. Jake's mom, Threadgill, in the room. Daisy lifting up her skirt. Daisy's vagina.

He could not look at the screen. And he could not look at his mom. He thought he would die if he saw his mom's face. So he focused on Threadgill's knee, bouncing up and down, nervously. The knee, more than the video, made Jake want to throw up. The knee, even more than the video, felt perverted.

It was horrible. The worst day of his life, until the next one. Worse than anything he'd been able to imagine. But the most awful part had already happened. It was between first and second period, even before the hideousness in Threadgill's office, and Jake had been heading out of the building and toward the gym, still believing the whole thing might blow over, still pretending to himself like it had never happened, blurring the edges of what he knew and what he hoped, when he saw Daisy Cavanaugh for the first time ever in school. He saw her down the hall.

She was autographing baseball bats. Some of the kids on the team had brought them to her as a goof. They were taking pictures of her with their cell phones and she was posing. Until she saw him. Daisy Cavanaugh in her too-tight jeans and her UGG boots, one hip jutted out, a hand on that hip, smiling broadly for the camera. Daisy Cavanaugh with too much eye makeup.

When she saw him her eyes gaped open like endless holes, ragged and raw, like two wounds that would never heal. Jake felt vertigo just looking at them, like if he got too close he, too, could fall down that well of pain into hopeless misery. He was the creator of her torment and he knew it. At that moment, inside him the twin ruling deities of the rest of his life, a giddy recognition of his own powers and a crushing sense of shame, were born. Both paled before the desire to save himself.

Daisy looked at him and stuck out her tongue.

"Thanks a lot," she said. Her voice was trembling.

Then whatever had opened up inside her closed over, and she went back to signing bats. Giving the people what they wanted.

She was famous now. *He'd* made her famous. She was autographing the bats and smiling a big, broad, winning smile.

O<small>NCE, IIE WAS A</small> golden boy.

Now he is a golden man. Handsome, smart, silver-haired Richard, Richard at forty-five, still with the tight abs and runner's legs, Richard in the hound's-tooth sport coat and black jeans, the clean white shirt, self-made Richard with his preternaturally cool, casual, youthful elegance. He is on the phone. He is on the phone with his distraught wife, Lizzie, in the middle of one of the most important meetings of his career, and he remains calm. For most of his life, Richard Bergamot has been allergic to failure. He isn't about to allow for a reversal of fortune now.

He sits with one hand curling around his BlackBerry, the left one, with the simple gold wedding band, those long "piano" fingers, his father's old Timex encircling his wrist for luck, his leather chair swiveling just enough to face away from the eclectic group of enemies and advocates it has taken him so many months of careful diplomacy to assemble, but not enough to relinquish his authority and control.

How can I possibly walk out now? Richard thinks, as he peers sideways at the gathering through long, dark lashes—they grow so ridiculously thick at times they actually obscure his vision; they "flutter" when he blinks. This is a phenomenon Richard has grown used to, although as a kid he'd trimmed them back with a nail scissors, sick of hearing the ladies at his church stage-whisper, "Wasted on a boy."

"Been dipping into the interferon again?" Lizzie teased the first time they slept together.

It has taken a great deal of calibrated effort to get all parties to agree to this sit-down—the West Harlem Development Corporation, the community activists, the whining college students, the coiffed wives of philanthropists, the local Parents' Association, Richard's own team of experts—and an endless amount of cajoling and arm-twisting to persuade Bertram Anderson, the senior assemblyman, to donate his Harlem offices for the purpose of this meeting (which is key, the location of this meeting is key); and yet it has all been done. These seemingly Herculean tasks have been completed.

The various warring factions are now present and assembled peaceably in Bert's conference room, around his long, chipped wooden table, with the rather worn black leather chairs that swivel (good thing), the wilting flowers, sweaty water glasses, and bound copies of all of Richard's charts and agendas and projections, the PowerPoint presentation, the computer that goes wherever Richard goes, like a lapdog or an ancillary lobe of his brain. There is a low-level scent of activity in the air, the musky respiration of skin mixed with the aroma of various perfumes and deodorants; it is the olfactory background hum of meetings when they get going, and Richard noted its presence about an hour in, as a positive barometrical measurement of the assembly's charge. No one was sweating profusely, no one was hot under the collar, there was no angry human stink.

Richard had been halfway through the presentation when he received the call, and now, as he is listening to his distraught wife, it is quickly becoming clear that he has been thrust into battle on not one but two fronts: (a) work, which he is prepared for, naturally; and (b) this thing with his kid, which he decidedly is not.

He is senior executive vice chancellor of the Astor University of the City of New York, and at the onset of the meeting he'd welcomed everyone individually and by name (prepping himself with Google Images the night before), thanking the skeptical, smug assemblyman for allowing them to gather in his offices, blowing a little sunshine up Bert's ass as he went. From the get-go, Richard did his best to set the group at ease. He poured the water himself, passing glasses around the table. He'd taken off his jacket and rolled up his sleeves, keeping it casual and friendly, biting into a donut off a plate of baked goods proffered by his deputy, George Strauss, before he'd even begun. In private, he is too vigilant to indulge in sweets—his father died of a coronary at forty-nine—but nothing puts off other people more than public displays of discipline. A little confectioners' sugar had sprinkled onto Richard's lap as he ate, and so he'd started to speak to the group with castdown eyes—those lashes again—casually brushing the powder off with his hand.

"Welcome, everyone," he'd said. "Here's a concept to em-

brace: no sugar donuts when wearing black jeans." He looked
up. "Here's a better one: let's take a rare, underutilized industrial
area in the greatest city in the world and turn it into a state-of-
the-art cohort campus to a first-tier university while creating jobs,
schools, and affordable housing for the surrounding community."
He'd put the half-eaten donut aside on his napkin for emphasis.

"Anyone who can accomplish the latter deserves the rest
of that donut, Richard," Bert said. A portly man in his sixties
with a dusting of silver gray in his well-trimmed beard, Bert, to
Richard, always looks like he has just come in out of the snow.
Born and bred in Harlem, Bert has run the district for the last
twenty-five years. He is as smart as and/or smarter than Richard,
perhaps wilier, by virtue of Richard's own rigorously honest as-
sessment. "Lying to yourself gets you nowhere," Richard's father
always said, so Richard does his best to adhere to that axiom.
Bert wears his experience and his legislative weight the way he
wears his signature well-tailored gold-buttoned vest. Snugly.
With gravitas.

The senior assemblyman is today's linchpin. If Richard can
get Bert's support, the rest will follow suit, eventually. The few
real estate holdouts they can always buy out at a premium. Richard has a slush fund set aside just for this purpose.

"I tell you what, Bert, when we're done here today, I'll split
it with you," Richard had said, earlier, before the call, nodding
playfully at the donut.

Manhattanville, east of Broadway and commercial Harlem,
consists of mostly warehouses and parking garages, windswept
river views, rubble-strewn lots, some auto body shops and gas
stations—there is presently so little foot traffic that often in good

weather some of the handful of proprietors and residents sit outside in the middle of the empty sidewalks on folding chairs, playing dominos on portable card tables. The neighborhood, if one can call it that, is home to La Floridad, the Cuban restaurant where Lizzie gets her café con leche en route to picking up the car (theirs is the cheapest garage in the city, and an expression of some residual shared frugality—they are both products of working-class families); Fairway Uptown, where she shops on Saturday mornings; and some of the most beautiful, antique iron latticework, huge trestles that—miraculously, considering their copious rot, those rusted stanchions—still manage to support the elevated subway line. The best landmark of all is a mysterious aerial road to nowhere that abruptly ends near the river where it meets up against the sky. On Richard's maps, it is an abandoned arm of the West Side Highway, but in his mind that graceful, castoff celestial boulevard is the "Stairway to Heaven" that he slow-danced to so many times as a kid. (He hears Jimmy Page's electric guitar riffing in his head every time he walks beneath it.)

Gazing up at the clouds through that intricate, corroded metalwork feels like peering through a veil of muddied silver lace, and the poetry of it all appeals to Richard, although once the university breaks ground the thing will have to go—unless he can turn it into a park, a green oasis, like the one a variety of developers plan for the High Line, the elevated railway that runs like a spine through the rough-and-tumble neighborhood of gas stations and art galleries in Chelsea, downtown. The possibilities here are endless! The pitfalls, myriad. Ergo, the complex, exhilarating joy of his job.

Best, for all its raw, physical gifts, this most western reach of

Harlem is virtually uninhabited—for New York, that is. Not that many people actually live there.

In the nine months Richard has spearheaded the university's plans to expand by building a new campus in Manhattanville, he has aimed to please, sensitive as he is to the university's missteps almost four decades prior, when their efforts to build new dorms and an indoor stadium ended in race riots. It is important that they do this right. Richard has said this over and over again. First to Lizzie, when he was being wooed away from Cornell and was contemplating taking the job, late one night, after sex, when they did their best talking, when she wasn't anxious and he was loose, when the breeze off the gorge was damp and sultry and the kids were asleep and the intense pleasure of living hovered over a waterfall that way—the music of it—was almost enough to make him spring naked to his feet, his dick still hard and wet, and pick up the phone and wake up the university's chief operating officer in New York and say, no, no, I am too fucking happy here to risk changing my life. Lizzie had slipped on her skirt and T-shirt from off of the floor, and said, "Let's sit on the porch; it's such a beautiful night," looking through the open window next to their bed. Outside, they'd talked, it seemed, for hours; he'd felt the need to make it clear to her that this job was about doing good—Lizzie liked that—that the challenge turned him on for sure, but that there was a vision here he'd like to fulfill. There was something about that night, the conversation, the excitement of this new venture, her willingness to give him what he wanted, that made him feel like he had when he'd first met her, unbeatable and unstoppable. Here was this smart, pretty girl eager to be his audience, witty but vulnerable; it was that vulnerability that always got to him. It amazed him that she was still ready to go with him where he wanted to go. It was his mission to make it worth her while. And so he says this often: "The university will expand correctly." It is as if, if he says it enough, it will become true.

To back this up, he is prepared to spend $150 million of the *university's* money (Lizzie loves to verbally insert the italics) over the next sixteen years to ensure not only the preservation but also the growth of the surrounding community as they build a campus that will catapult the university into the new century. He is in possession of a big fat economic gift, a gift he can give to Harlem; Richard firmly believes this. He never would have accepted the position if he did not. Richard is a dyed-in-the-wool Populist. His father was a postal worker. His mother, a homemaker. The youngest of three sons, he was the first in his family to graduate from high school. What had once only been simply fact, the architecture of Richard's life, even in his own mind, has been elevated to myth.

It is Richard's mission to persuade the members of his audience to see what he sees, that Manhattanville is ripe for development, that developing Manhattanville will not only increase the academic, artistic, and economic reach of the university but, in doing so, will also cast significant academic, artistic, and economic light on the surrounding neighborhood, enhancing it without gentrifying it (gentrifying it *too much*, he qualifies internally; a little gentrification is good, he reasons: banks, drugstores, supermarkets, jobs) or destroying it. This is called "city planning."

So Richard began this morning the way he always begins, by stating his objectives simply and directly. (With Jake he'd say,

"Today you are going to clean up your room," and then list a vast array of directives: "You will make the bed and change the linens. You will cull through and straighten out your dresser drawers. You will attack that mess on your desk and make sense of it. You will alphabetize your underwear, my underwear, and the dog's underwear," the last delivered with a grin and a noogie—there was no dog—and then the two of them would end up wrestling on the floor.) He'd then proceed to get as wonkish and as detailed as possible, dazzling his audience with data, bringing them to their intellectual knees. As he outlined the various stages in the development of Manhattanville, Richard did what he did best: he delegated, he delegated, and then jumped in (that is, he interrupted politely, self-effacingly, bursting with enthusiasm, as if he could barely contain his excitement) with a flurry of addendums, proving himself as expert as the army of experts he has scattered around the table. He has seated his team strategically among the community activists, the philanthropists, the local apparatchik, the assemblyman and his aides.

"No 'us versus them,'" Richard had warned prior to the meeting. "We are one, guys. A single human organism."

This morning, he'd called upon his colleagues on a first-name basis, no matter how accomplished or renowned ("Here's where you come in, Marcus," and "Maria, take it away"), as he proceeded point by PowerPoint throughout his talk—employing the architects and their computer-enhanced drawings, representatives from the School of Education to discuss the new Public Intermediate School that was a keystone of their proposal; the head of Relocation Services was there, too, Luz Esquilar, with her background in finance and social work (Yale Law), to talk about moving the few actual residents of "inarguably underutilized and industrial" Manhattanville into comparable or better housing for the same dollar or less. (How they really were going to accomplish that move in this real estate market was one of the sticky issues that Richard chewed over and over again. He had his eye on several buildings in Hamilton and Washington Heights, East Harlem—not Harlem, exactly, but close. Was it close enough? he wondered.) Richard had his whole team at the ready to run through their spiels, their words of comfort and renewal, their battle cry for change and opportunity and a new order, when he'd noticed his phone whirring on the conference table.

Lizzie had had the wherewithal to text him first. Richard was laughing along with the rest of them at one of his own jokes ("Is it time to eat the donut, Bert?") and glanced down and saw the word *URGENT* on the screen of his phone. When they'd first arrived, all the members of the meeting had rested their phones on the table like a bunch of gunslingers sitting at a bar. "Surrender your weapons," Richard had said jovially when he'd joined them. He'd not hesitated one millisecond in taking Lizzie's call when the phone vibrated again. He was calm, but tabloid headlines did a ticker-tape crawl along the bottom substrata of his thoughts. Often, when asked about his ability to multitask, the image that reaches Richard first is the post-9/11 screen on CNN. He is capable of entertaining several fractured narratives at once.

Lizzie would not interrupt him unless she had to. And Richard Bergamot, by definition, is the kind of man who takes his wife's "urgent" phone call in the middle of a high-powered meeting— he is a family man. That's what the articles say about him, and it is true. Phi Beta Kappa at Princeton, Stanford MBA and PhD in

Econ. He is the kind of guy (even as a kid) who always has a clean shirt, in his briefcase or his locker. It was the clean shirt that got him started—he worked after school and summers in a fast-food restaurant slinging Macho Burritos in San José, and the wardrobe of pristine white polo shirts beneath his uniform impressed the franchise owner, who'd sent his own rather feckless boy back east to boarding school. "The rich rule the world; you better learn how to deal with them early," Mr. Harrison said, and so he guided Richard through the application process, helping him negotiate a free ride.

St. Paul's paved Richard's pathway to Princeton, where he became interested in finance, all those wealthy prep school friends of his tempting him with the grace and ease of their gracious, easy lives. At Stanford he remembered his roots, inspired by his thesis advisor, vowing to live a life of public service—public service with money. He was a golden boy who grew up to be a golden man, a family man. Richard Bergamot loves his family. All his ambition and striving is in service to that love.

So when he hears the tremulous tone in his wife's voice as she struggles to convey the information that sounds as if it is rapidly whirling inside her head, he tries very hard to brush away his impatience. Lizzie isn't making sense.

"He's physically all right?" Richard asks. "Yes, yes," Lizzie says. "But honey, they are suspending him. They want us to come up to school and get him right away."

She anxiously tries to explain something about Jake and an email, a love letter, the school, suspension, the poor, poor mother of that pitiable little girl . . . Richard jotting down notes on his legal pad as she rambles: *Turn the meeting over to Bert, Power-*

Point presentation to Kate, meet L.B. at the garage, and his father's most cogent axiom: *Don't ever let them see you sweat . . .* He
actually writes this down. Jotting notes gives Richard something
to do and confers upon his reluctant audience an aura of significance to the phone call. Richard looks around the boardroom,
at the polite but impatient faces—busy, important people, all of
them—turning away from him now and toward each other in a
Kabuki-like effort to offer him some false modicum of privacy.
He does not want to leave this meeting before he's won them over.

Ironically, Richard's garage, MTP (the initials stand for More
Than Parking—"What more?" said Lizzie. "Bikini waxes?"), is
located in Manhattanville, and is also one of the first businesses
slated to be turned over to the university because the university,
as of six months ago, under Richard's tutelage, is now MTP's
landlord. It was one of Richard's first acquisitions. The garage
is a fifteen-minute sprint from the assemblyman's 125th Street
offices—five minutes if Richard can catch a cab, which is not
always possible on 125th Street. Maybe a car service, or a gypsy,
but you can't count on a yellow taxi, not yet, not until the arrival
of the Manhattanville campus, that is—which leaves him with
very little time to extricate himself from this meeting, if extricat-
ing is indeed what he is going to do. Certainly this is what his
wife is asking for.

He lets Lizzie go on, because she needs to; it is always wiser to
let her perseverate a little, if time allows (she is more logical and
reasonable once she's had a chance to "talk it out"), before weigh-
ing in. Usually he likes to help her; it makes him feel good. But in
the moment, *his* moment, he feels a brief surge of annoyance—why
can't she just handle this? Still, there is no time for irritation now;

he loves her, he is her husband, it's their boy they are discussing, and he needs to settle her down.

"The secret of Richard's success is a cool head," Lizzie always says, wryly, out of the corner of her lovely mouth, when one friend or another marvels at Richard's latest accomplishment, or at some dinner thrown in his honor. She compliments him in public with pride, but pride with an edge, like so many married women of her generation, because she isn't totally above a little jealousy. She isn't 100 percent above feeling envious of his stature, she admits, even when she counts upon it, quality-of-life-wise. She hasn't accomplished all she's wanted to accomplish, she confesses repeatedly, after a glass or two of wine, publicly leaking her neurosis, what with her PhD, her two kids, her tug-of-war between the family and the workplace, dipping in and out of academia, the occasional bones Cornell threw her, a class here, a symposium there, before running back to the kids. Who wouldn't like that kind of freedom? Richard sometimes thinks when he stays late at the office, Lizzie calling to remind him of the importance of face time with the family. Men were never allowed the space to mull over whether they wanted to work—they just worked, period. What she admires most about Richard, Lizzie always says when she has officially drunk too much, is the fact that he isn't conflicted—he is a straight and independent arrow tirelessly shooting toward success.

So let me accomplish something here, today, Richard thinks. Lizzie, honey, don't make me fuck this up.

Jake and the girl are teenagers. Teenagers flirt and embarrass themselves. They are biologically programmed to do so. Wasn't he young once, too? How big a deal could this be? When he was a teenager he thought about sex all day long. Even while he was getting some, he was thinking about when he could get some next.

Richard looks up and catches the eye of the smug, self-satisfied young community organizer, Steven Schwartz, a graduate of the university, recently a teenager himself. Is *he* getting any? Schwartz has a slightly schlubby young Bolshevik edge, via Williamsburg. A goatee and a shaved head. Ten extra pounds. Richard is a quarter century older than this kid, but he carries about a third of his body fat. Schwartz brought up the term "eminent domain" at the start of the meeting: a pre-emptive strike. His shoulders shaking with postadolescent rage and barely contained excitement—jumping the gun, tone-deaf to the rhythms and parries of a well-timed and executed assault. Even Bert had glared at the kid; Richard assumed the assemblyman had wanted to launch that particular salvo himself at the proper moment in the charged, fast-paced allegro of the post-presentation Q&A. Richard gives that fucker Schwartz a cool smile and a nod. Richard raises his right forefinger. One minute, he'll be off the phone in one minute. He hates being forced off his game.

"Sweetheart, this sounds like typical teen stuff," he says into the phone when Lizzie asks if he can meet her at the car.

"You mean you're not going to come?" she says, hope deflating out of her voice like a loss of pride.

There is silence.

She is his wife. She knows him. As much as anyone knows anyone.

Lizzie says, "Fine. I'll pick him up, and I'll have Jakey apolo-

gize to the girl and her parents—" and now it is his turn to interrupt her. Richard does not want his son apologizing for anything,
not yet.

"No," he says, authoritatively. "We'll sort this all out together
at home." He whispers, "Just get him the hell out of there." Then
he says the next part clearly enough for his audience to hear him
signing off. "See you later, honey."

"Okay," says Lizzie, sounding a little less desperate. Either
Richard has successfully talked her down or she is wisely giving
up and beginning to orchestrate her own next move.

That is her problem. He has his.

Richard needs to take his meeting back. He puts the phone
down and instinctively reaches for a live grenade.

"Steven brought up the words *eminent domain* at the start of
our meeting," Richard says, with a nod toward the fat kid in the
corner, "for which I'm grateful. So let's talk frankly now about the
elephant in the room."

After the meeting is over Richard feels amazingly light. The
spring breeze is cool against his neck, his collar blessedly open.
As these things go, the whole day has gone swimmingly. He has
layered down a foundation of promise and goodwill, building the
groundwork for consensus, a strong basis for moving forward.
He remembers how he outmaneuvered Steven Schwartz so that
even the boy, sputtering with free-floating, inarticulate rage, understood he was behaving like a clown. "White privilege," said
Schwartz. "Culturally insensitive . . ."

"Take a closer look at the proposals, Steven," Richard said

patiently, passing him piles of paper. "The education will be top-notch and inclusive—it's a new and exciting option for the neighborhood kids as well as Astor U. families—which are as diverse a group as any you can find in New York." Here he shook his head a little. "It's a bit antiquated to assume our faculty is homogeneous . . ."

Now Richard feels like he is floating in his skeleton, taller, stronger, and more alive, lambent; this is the way he always feels after a significant achievement. It is the sensation itself, he sometimes thinks, that he is addicted to. He tries to preserve it as he walks back to his apartment, perhaps not as quickly as the situation with Jake warrants (the situation suggests a cab, a car service, a subway; a phone call stating, "I'm on my way home, honey"). But the moment consists of a rare fusion of solitude and satisfaction, and he isn't quite ready to surrender it just yet.

At home, in the kitchen, both his wife and son will be in need of shoring up. There will be phone calls to make, parents to placate, school administrators to stroke or to intimidate, he isn't sure which tactic to take yet. During the meeting, Richard had been the executive vice chancellor of the Astor University of the City of New York; at home he will be "the dad," the husband. The responsibilities of these roles are enormous. Right now, in the intermission between acts, he has no part to play. He belongs to no one. He feels good. He wants to preserve that feeling for a while longer.

Richard decides to crisscross through the projects, making his way toward Broadway, soaking up the cool sunshine, deftly sidestepping little logs of dog shit and slaloming through the garbage that tumbles out of the overflowing bins and wafts through

the spring breeze as if it has wings. There are teenagers gathered in the small prison run of a playground, listening to loud
music. Making out. Two fat old ladies sit on a park bench, the
flesh around their knees overhanging their support hose. Laundry dangles from lines off the little rusting terraces. The air
smells like fried food. It is a smell that once made him salivate
and now makes him gag. There are so many people outdoors in
the middle of the day you'd think this was the weekend. Doesn't
anyone around here have a job? School? They need Richard and
his programs and his progress.

He nods at a man with a gold front tooth. The guy's arm muscles, which look carved out of ebony, are resplendent beneath
his sawed-off sweatshirt. There is more skin than shirt here, and
Richard thinks if he had that physique himself he'd want to flaunt
it, too. He really should be lifting heavier weights.

The meeting went well, extraordinarily so. The local school
board representatives were particularly impressed. Schwartz be
damned—Who doesn't want better schools for their children?
Richard thinks, and for a moment, in an uncharacteristic excess
of self-esteem and ambition, he allows himself the indulgence of
contemplating what he could accomplish if he were someday to
take over the New York City School System perhaps, or the university itself . . . Once the Manhattanville operation is in full swing
the sky will be the limit in terms of his future employment. Public
or private sector. This might be the time to make real money.

Just twenty minutes ago Bert himself put a hand on Richard's
shoulder and said, "If you can pull half of this off, we're all in
better shape up here, just as long as no one is forced from their
homes, son." He'd called Richard "son." Bert is one sharp cookie,

instinctively zeroing in on his Achilles' heel, Richard's lingering hunger for his own dead father. It was a vote of confidence and a warning, and Richard vows to heed it, at least as long as it is possible and prudent to do so.

He suddenly feels a light, pulsating pressure on his shoulder, right where Bert had touched him more firmly; it is like the massaging fingers of a Japanese hostess, featherlike, goose-bump-giving, reverberating through his bones with a dangerous chill racing through his synapses and up to his teeth. He whirls around—it had been imprudent for him, a well-dressed white guy carrying a computer, to wander through the projects. What an imbecile! Is it the dude with the muscles? Richard is instantly in fight-or-flight mode, adrenaline pumping. It takes only a second to realize his situation and laugh out loud. This will be the last time he hears his own laughter in weeks.

The tremor he feels is his BlackBerry, once again set on vibrate. He'd shoved it into his interior sport jacket pocket after Lizzie's earlier call, and that pocket is now resting on his shoulder.

He reaches in and pulls out the phone. Clicks On without bothering to verify the caller and says, "I'm on my way. I'll be home in ten minutes, honey."

There is silence on the line.

"I want you to be an asshole," Lizzie says.

In all the years he has known her, Richard has never heard Lizzie sound like this before. Harsh, strategic, uncompromising. Like she is declaring war. Like she is declaring war on anyone and everyone who has threatened their child. Like he, Richard, is the general who has to fight it.

I want you to be an asshole.

Richard thinks back, back to all the years when Lizzie wanted him *not* to be an asshole, when she questioned his humanity, worried that life and work were changing him, making him hard, turning him cold. Where was the caring, compassionate visionary she'd married? she'd ask him wryly from time to time. Then she'd gently nudge him back on track. It was one of the reasons he'd picked her: she made him a better person. Who will Richard be if Lizzie, of all people, gives him permission to be an animal? Without her reining him in, how far will Richard go?

Now Lizzie *wants* him to be an asshole.

He will give her what she wants.

They are in the lawyer's offices, one o'clock. Wednesday afternoon, Jake looking almost comical in a too-large blue blazer and one of Richard's ties. The boy's limbs are long and gangly and they hang awkwardly from his torso as he slumps down into the plush leather chair. The cuffs of his white shirt rattle around his forearms like bangles. He's still got that dumb string thing tied around one wrist; Richard makes a mental note to cut it off when they get home.

The conference table is long and burnished. The wood so rich and dark it glistens; it's been deeply oiled and it looks like the surface might ripple to the touch. The boy leans forward and stares at his reflection in the shiny wood. With his neck bent that way—like a crane swooping down for a drink—his head appears bigger, weightier, more orbicular and bobbling than it ever has before. Jake seems to Richard to be too skinny and too tall and too small in that chair, all at the same time.

He doesn't fit his own frame, and his frame doesn't fit the seat. He looks almost spindly, as if his arms and legs could be blown around like a weathervane. The knot of his tie is off-center. It's Richard's tie: a dark blue silk with a thin turquoise stripe—a little schmancy maybe, Lizzie said, for the venue, but the most youthful one in Richard's closet. No matter how many times Richard or Lizzie has reached over to straighten it today, it invariably lists left again.

Richard had tied that knot himself, and he'd had a moment when he did so, standing behind his son in front of the bathroom mirror that morning—Jake looking for a second like the Hindu god Vishnu, with all those multiple arms. That's how Richard's own father had taught him; Dad could only tie a tie as if he were performing the ritual upon himself, and so Dad had stood behind Richard, as he had both of Richard's older brothers before him, and it hadn't occurred to Richard to teach Jake any other way. While he was adjusting the knot, Richard had suddenly noticed how truly broad Jake's shoulders had become. Like a wire frame hanger from which the rest of his lean body simply hung.

Richard had teared up a little then, and the boy had taken notice. "I'm sorry, Dad," said Jake, his eyes muddy swollen green, like a pond all stirred up after a series of summer storms.

"It wasn't a smart thing to do, was it?" Richard said.

"I didn't know, I didn't realize, I had no idea, Dad . . ." Jake said. "I didn't think."

"That's the problem," said Richard. "You have to think. You always have to think."

"It was a mistake, Richard," said Lizzie, from the doorway. Neither of them had seen her standing there. She was in her

"Richard's interview suit," a black Armani she'd bought in Ithaca, on eBay, to charm the provost and the COO, with stockings, low heels, and lipstick; her wavy auburn hair slicked back in a French twist. "Jake would never intentionally hurt anyone. He couldn't possibly have known what would happen—"

"You should never send an email you don't want the whole world to see. How many times have I said that?" said Richard.

"She asked for it," Lizzie cut in. "She made the video, she emailed it—what would Dr. Freud say," she said, shaking her head. "That poor, wretched, stupid girl. Marjorie says the mother's always away somewhere, that even when she was little she was always picked up by a nanny." Her eyes met Richard's in the mirror. "He needs to shave, Richard."

"He can do that himself," said Richard. "He needs a haircut."

"My hair?" said Jake. It had taken forever for it to grow this long.

"Short," said Richard. "So your ears stick out."

"I still can't believe they made us watch that thing together in Treadwell's office." Lizzie stole a look at Jake, and then whispered, "Did I tell you, she waxed? Down there . . ."

Richard felt the skin on his face tighten. Whether it was because Lizzie was being inappropriate in front of Jake or because she'd bungled it so big time at Wildwood, he wasn't sure. He honestly wasn't sure why he felt so angry.

"You shouldn't have agreed to it," said Richard.

"I was trying to work with the school," said Lizzie. There was both incredulity and a little heat on her words.

"There is no working with the school," said Richard.

"I know that now, Richard," said Lizzie firmly. "I wonder

if you, too, would have realized it in the moment had you been there."

Her brown eyes met his green ones in the mirror—no surprise Jake's were the color of algae. She did not have the right to chastise him, especially in front of their son. Richard had been at work; he'd been supporting the family. And then it was as if their argument played out in the short form telepathically: they volleyed back and forth from eyes to eyes locked in the mirror, marital shorthand from years of experience, one upping the ante, testing to see who would concede this time, and indeed it seemed that in this instance Richard had won. Because Lizzie got a little softer then. She thought he was right, maybe; or she was timing her battles; maybe she was just gearing up for the big one, a more important confrontation that would inevitably come; maybe she wanted to protect Jake; maybe she just knew Richard enough to recognize a good moment to back down. Whatever it was, their dispute played out rapid-fire and died out.

This was marriage, Richard thought, pragmatically compressed into emotional haiku.

"They could have turned it all into a teaching moment," Lizzie said. "A school is supposed to help children and their families, by definition a school—"

"If he were eighteen he could be charged with disseminating child pornography," said Richard, and instantly regretted it. He sounded like a robot and he knew it. He didn't want to fight now, either. But someone had to assess the situation, assess it properly, keep cool. And once again, it seemed that responsibility was his. He'd been on the phone, the Internet. He'd begun his due diligence. He'd already talked to lawyers. The video had found its way to a music-sharing website—that is, one of the kids had sent it, thank God not Jake; Richard grilled him every way to Sunday, and Jake swore he had not posted it, because that could lead to further legal woes—and it had reached thousands, if not hundreds of thousands. Possibly it had already reached a million viewers. A million. The staggering consequence of a flick of his son's index finger, the amazing irrevocable reach of his unleashed power—it was sort of stunning, really, what his son could actually do.

Kids have fucked up before, Richard thought, again and again. Kids have fucked up since time immemorial. It is their biological mandate to fuck up, Richard repeated to himself inside his own head. But not like this. Up until now, there was an element of containment to their fuck-ups. You could keep it to yourself pretty much and pay to have the rest swept away.

"McHenry is seventeen," said Jake, looking like he might be sick. "Luke is eighteen," he said slowly.

Lizzie looked at Jake with an inspector's gaze.

"I'll shave him," said Lizzie.

"I'll do it myself, Mom," said Jake. His eyes were brimming, but he held those broad shoulders square.

Which now accounts for the two red scratches on his peachy face. The marinelike haircut. His ears twitching on both sides of his head like a fawn's. Richard had marched Jake into a Latino barbershop on Amsterdam after he'd called into the office. "Not a buzz, but almost as short." Richard stayed to watch as the long chestnut locks hit the linoleum in graceful spirals, like streamers the day after the party. He had nothing better to do this morning. Yesterday he'd gone into work. Yesterday Richard had "tried to set the gears in motion to make good on the goodwill of the meeting," but it had been a lost cause. Yesterday he'd still had some stupid, ridiculous hope that this thing might actually die down.

All morning Richard's BlackBerry and his landline had rung like crazy. His email, his IM were going nuts. Yesterday, Lizzie dropped Coco off at school in the a.m. as per usual, but he had had to pick her up in the afternoon, because Lizzie called him midday semi-hysterically and said she didn't want to leave Jake alone at home, the poor kid was torturing himself, and she just couldn't face the scene, again, that day, at pickup. Everyone was buzzing, she said. Everyone wanted to have coffee. Everyone wanted to talk. "No one ever wanted to have coffee before," said Lizzie. "They want the dirt," she said. "They want to trash-talk *that girl.*"

She gave him a list of instructions: arrive at 2:45, and the kindergarten class will be assembled on the sidewalk and half of them will already have left and he won't have to kibitz with anyone. Also: "Bring a snack for Coco, she'll need protein first, not sugar, so a nut bar or a squeezy yogurt; you can pick up a mini-ham-and-cheese at the foodie place on the corner with the big windows, unless you are trying to avoid people . . ." And then: "Poor Jake; the kid is curled up on the couch like a worm. I hate that girl."

It wasn't Richard's style to hide. He'd arrived on time and sauntered across the sidewalk, nodding a bright hello at almost anyone who looked vaguely familiar, and swung Coco up up up into the air and then onto the royal perch of his shoulders. "It's my dad," shouted Coco, in utter amazement. She bellowed this into the crowd. "It's my dad," as if he'd materialized out of thin air. When he heard her squeal of delight, Richard realized he'd never picked his daughter up from school in the city before. In Ithaca, Coco would come back with him up the hill to his office on Tuesdays and Thursdays, when Lizzie taught that grad seminar on Goncharova, Picasso, and Braque. Sometimes he'd let Coco run loose on the Arts Quad, glancing out his window from time to time to make sure she wasn't annoying any of the lounging undergrads and keeping them from their seductions or their studies. But in New York, pickup had been her mother's purview.

Richard dropped Coco off at Wildwood Lower, also a somewhat rare occurrence, that very morning, and Lizzie arranged for a playdate for after school. Sydney, "Clementine's mother," had called the day before. Lizzie had actually picked up as Sydney was leaving a message. Usually she screened, and if it was someone she wanted to talk to, Lizzie called back later. Who was Sydney? Who was Clementine? Did it matter? With Coco safely tucked away at some banker's duplex on Park Avenue, neither parent would have to face the perp walk at pickup, and as an added bonus, they wouldn't have to worry about the time while in their newfound attorney's offices, except in terms of billable hours.

"That was so nice," Lizzie had said, after she'd hung up the phone. "Sydney said Jake is an innocent. She said they are all innocents, the girl, too. She said the parents were richer than God and out to lunch and that poor kid had been left to raise herself. Rich, but deprived, you know?"

"So she blamed the girl's parents?" Richard said.

"Yes, no, I don't know," said Lizzie. "What I liked was that she didn't blame us." She paused, thinking. "And that she reached out. She's the only one who has so far, Richard. In a real way."

So Coco was taken care of for the afternoon. They'd borrowed the blazer from Marjorie for Jake to wear to the attorney's office, and Lizzie had ventured out long enough to pick it up from Marjorie's doorman. The two mothers had been on the phone all afternoon and all night and then again all morning. Henry was in trouble, but seemingly less trouble than Jake. Lizzie seemed to think there was safety in numbers. According to Marjorie, the girl's parents had pulled her out of school for the remaining weeks of the semester and had arranged for her to take her final exams off campus. They were contemplating (a) a move to their home in Saint-Paul de Vence, or a move to their home on Martha's Vineyard; (b) relocating temporarily to their apartment in Cyprus; (c) sticking Daisy in one of the all-girls academies for next year, or maybe boarding school; (d) suing the boys and Wildwood and anyone else they could think of; or (e) all of the above.

Richard had spent the whole afternoon and evening the day before pulling in favors, tracking down legal representation. He was amazed at the recommendations he'd gotten: Thomas P. Puccio, lawyer for Alex Kelly, a rapist punk from Connecticut who'd attacked a girl from his high school on the way home from a party, jumped bail, and fled to Europe to ski for seven years before returning to face the music; Jack T. Litman, the scumbag who had represented Robert Chambers, the "Preppie Killer," a heroin addict who'd strangled a classmate while having "rough sex" in Central Park. How could anyone think Jake fell into this category?

Through one of the university's legal team, Richard found someone circumspect, from a blue-chip firm: Sean O'Halloran.

"I've got a sixteen-year-old boy myself," said O'Halloran, over the phone. "Sends shivers down my spine."

Richard had called into the office first thing this morning—a family matter, he'd said to his secretary, although the story had already broken on the Internet, and Marjorie's spies said there were TV news helicopters and reporters this morning up at Wildwood. Richard had contacted the COO the day before, prior to beginning his legal research. It was imperative that his boss hear the news from Richard himself. Theirs had been a terse, businesslike conversation. The COO said, "Do what you can to defuse this thing." This morning Richard sent a follow-up email. He would call later in the day, he typed with his thumbs on his BlackBerry, to apprise the university fully of the situation. Best to get a legal handle first before making his pitch to the COO.

Richard hoped to keep his name out of the papers—his son is a minor after all, although he doubted the older boys would be given the same courtesy—but that, too, now seems like a lost cause. It is already up on the Internet. The question is: Did the powers that be at the university read the gossip sites Richard himself had not visited until today? And now that the COO knew, what could possibly keep him away? It was human nature, it seemed, to Google. Ridiculously tempting, highly addictive, a weakness of the flesh. Marjorie had called Lizzie with the news: "The kids made Gawker," and Lizzie passed that nugget on, hand over phone receiver, in stunned amazement, almost as if it were an accomplishment.

They sit around the mahogany table in O'Halloran's conference room. "Someone is giving a deposition in his office," his secretary said when she led the Bergamots apologetically to this wood-paneled book-lined room. For a moment, Richard compares the opulence of this meeting room to the one he presided over Monday; the rooms themselves living, breathing dioramas illustrating the differences between the public and the private sector. And then they wait. They wait and wait for O'Halloran. Richard never makes anyone wait if he can help it. But O'Halloran holds Richard's son's future in his hands. This is a little like waiting for a neurosurgeon, Richard thinks, and then stops the thought, blocks it. The analogy is too terrible and too frightening.

Jake is just a kid. He wiggles in his suit. He looks almost grown, but like a kid still anyway—he looks like he's not one or the other, but a baby somehow, and from certain angles, a man. Richard wasn't even tuned into the fact that his son had suddenly changed and seemed much older. Is he a virgin? At fifteen, almost sixteen, Richard wasn't. It hasn't even occurred to him until this moment that Jake could be having sex, the times are so different. Kids wait these days; they don't all do drugs (Lizzie informed him of this fact after a seminar she took at The Freedom Institute: "They told us sixty percent of kids today don't even experiment with anything," she said in amazement), and Richard hasn't bothered to turn to that channel yet. Just seconds ago it was Jake whom Richard was swinging up upon his shoulders. It was Jake shouting out joyfully, "It's my dad!" Jake and his friends seem so much younger to Richard than he was at their age—at this age Richard had worked his way away from home to boarding school; he'd wrangled himself a scholarship; he'd had a girlfriend at school with a diaphragm; her mother had taken her to see her own Beacon Hill gynecologist. He always carried a condom in his pocket. It sat next to the money he'd earned himself.

"Sean O'Halloran," O'Halloran says, entering the room. He is short, balding but red-haired, freckly and blue-eyed, well groomed and wearing a three-piece suit—exactly as he was in the photo Richard Googled. The secretary who escorted them into the room accompanies him. She's a nice-looking woman in her fifties. She wears a short strand of pearls. Perhaps Lizzie should be wearing pearls; Richard bought her some about fifteen years ago, slightly longer, that dipped gracefully just below her clavicle— throughout his childhood his mother had sighed from time to time over some magazine ad or other and said, "Someday I am going to buy myself a string of pearls"—but he'd rarely seen Lizzie wear them. Interviews and funerals. Dinner with the COO when he was being wooed for this job. But mostly the pearls sat in a jewelry box collecting dust on top of her dresser.

O'Halloran shakes Richard's hand and then Jake's—a nice move, Richard notes—and then he shakes Lizzie's. "Your father and I talked on the phone," O'Halloran says to Jake. "I don't want to waste anybody's time. You are in trouble. As far as I can tell, we have two areas to worry about, and the first is school. If we can get them to back down—"

"They've suspended him indefinitely," interrupts Lizzie. "And we're entering finals period. That means for every test he misses he gets a zero. He's in his sophomore year; he's an A student—"

"A's and B's, Mom," says Jake.

"This will destroy his chances of getting into college. Plus, I don't want this going down on his permanent record. Richard, do you think it will?"

Richard doesn't know. He is new to this. Whatever occurred didn't occur during school time or on school property. Still, they should probably be exploring the option of switching schools. But who would take Jake now? He feels a sense of bewilderment. Since when did anyone ever think of Jake as a troubled kid? Jake's whole life, Richard has been so proud of him. He reaches out a hand to pat Jake on the shoulder. Jake looks up gratefully, and Richard gives his shoulder a squeeze before he removes his hand.

O'Halloran continues: "The second potential problem is if the girl's parents choose to press charges."

"What about 'disseminating child pornography'?" says Richard. "Is he protected because he's underage?"

"We can discuss all of this later." O'Halloran nods at Jake. "We're going to need to know what happened. From start to finish, in your own words."

"Just tell the truth, honey," says Lizzie. She is talking to Jake but she stares at Richard.

"Leave nothing out," says Richard. "The girl came on to you, right? She sent the email to you. She never asked you not to forward it . . ."

Jake nods, looking from one parent to the other.

O'Halloran looks at the bookshelf. Richard notices that there is something funny about his eyes. There is a way in which they seem shut off; they emit no light. He almost looks like he's blind.

"When I was a kid," O'Halloran says, "I went to summer camp in the Catskills. Two of the kids took pictures of themselves naked—a girl and a boy. I guess we must have been younger than Jacob here, eleven or twelve, and the pictures, they were Polaroids back then, they got passed around the bunk and fell into the counselor's hands. The girl got sent home—she'd been caught doing something else earlier in the month, smoking or eating candy or something—it was so long ago, I honestly can't remember. I'd forgotten the whole episode until you called . . . The boy was put on probation. That was it. The rest was left up to their families' discretion."

"This *should* be a family matter," says Lizzie. "I still don't see why we can't work this all out privately."

O'Halloran turns toward Jake, his eyes still focused somehow on the distance. "I was that boy."

Jake smiles weakly.

"My father, he beat the shit out of me—excuse me." Here O'Halloran turns his head, not his gaze, to Lizzie; perhaps the problem is with his pupils. Maybe they've just been dilated? "He kicked my ass when I got home. But when my mother was out of the room he whispered in my ear, 'Chip off the old block.' "

Lizzie does not know how to react to this. Richard watches her fluctuate from grateful to amused to appalled. Her face is so expressive; it's always been as if he could read her mind. Richard's face is just the opposite. Once, not too long ago, Lizzie had queried, sort of as a joke, "What if all the time I think you are wrapped up in great thoughts, you're actually thinking about what you watched last night on television?" As if, if he said yes, the truth would prove that she had wasted her life. She often said, especially when they were younger, that she wished he would open up a little more, that he would put more trust in her, and he's certainly tried. But Richard is who he is, and over the years he's realized that Lizzie seems to value his "containment," for lack of a better word. It works for her. She, like Richard himself, sees his steadiness as something to rely upon.

"Kids are kids," says O'Halloran, with a shrug. "They do stupid stuff." He stares ahead. "The thing you guys don't understand is that with this email business, there is no such thing as confidentiality anymore."

Is he addressing Jake or is he addressing Lizzie? This gaze thing is driving Richard nuts. It's like visual fingernails on a chalkboard; it makes it impossible to connect with him. Richard did better with O'Halloran on the phone. He feels the urge to break something, a lamp or one of the decorative china bowls that sit in a line down the center of the table.

Jake nods, but he looks dumbfounded, like he doesn't get what O'Halloran is talking about at all. Richard doubts his son has ever thought about confidentiality as a concept.

The whole cab ride home, Lizzie talks to Richard. Jake has a window seat, and he has the window open, his face to the wind, like a dog would, like a golden retriever, his lips parted, mouth slightly open, tongue plush and pink.

"So what did you think?" says Lizzie. "Did you like him? I liked him, I think I liked him." She does not look sure.

"He's supposed to be good," says Richard. "The best."

"I know, but those eyes—they creeped me out. What's wrong with them? It's like he's blind or something."

Richard can't figure it out himself.

Lizzie brings a hand to her hair; curly wisps are flying out of her French twist. She tries to tuck them back.

"Why do you think he told us that story?" says Lizzie. "Was he trying to minimize the shame factor? Or maximize it? Is there still an operative shame factor, Richard? Or has the Internet killed all that? I mean, if everything that's private goes public, is it still humiliating?"

"It depends if the action itself is inherently shameful, Lizzie."

"Like 'furries'?" She is both listening and not listening to him. She gets like this sometimes. He pictures her mind like an old barn, her thoughts like swallows: all day long they swoop in and out.

"Furries?" Richard says.

"You know, those people who dress up like stuffed animals *to have sex*"—she mouths the last three words, but Jake's still staring out the window. "That article in *Vanity Fair*? The global network has set them free, Richard. Now they can find each other. Chat rooms. They have conventions and stuff. So is what they do shameful? Or just weird? If there's a lot of them, maybe it's not so weird at all?"

"Like pedophiles?" says Richard. "The purpose of shame is to curtail dangerous behavior."

She's sitting on the hump in the middle of the cab, knee pressed to knee but with her feet straddling the thing, and she leans over Jake and rolls the window up a bit. "Sorry, sweetie, but the wind is too blowy for me."

Jake sits back, the window now half closed. He stares out at the passing streets.

"Do you think O'Halloran was trying to be funny?" Lizzie says, the flight of her thoughts turning and banking. "Do you think he was trying to relate to Jake?" She pats Jake's shoulder for emphasis. "Do you think he was saying 'boys will be boys'? Do you think he was being sexist?"

Even with the window only partly open, the back draft blows some more of her hair out of place. A wisp falls into her mouth. She pushes it aside impatiently with a little articulated arpeggio of her fingers.

"Do you think he'll make things right for us?" she asks. She collapses back against the seat. She closes her eyes.

Jake doesn't look like he's listening at all, his eyes are shut too, and his mouth is open. He looks stoned.

With her eyes still closed, Lizzie says, "I wonder what this all will cost us, Richard?"

"Look," Richard says to the COO of the university, on the phone, "you can't stop progress. If we don't develop Manhattanville, it will be developed anyway. By the real estate guys. There's, like, nothing left on the island, and here's this great big uninhabited space. By business. What an opportunity! The residents are going to be forced out one way or another. Some of them will be; might as well have the area developed responsibly, by a world-class university, in the interest of science and scholarship, the pursuit of knowledge. Compassionately, Mike. With an eye on preserving and enhancing the existing community. We own most of this stuff already, and it's blighted—I've made sure it's blighted. We haven't renewed any leases. We shut down half the garage space—we're preserving it for Astor employees, by the way—we've evicted tenants, the illegal ones, you know, from the loft spaces near the river. Foot traffic is now less than zero. So we'll turn a blighted urban area into a university town. That's the skinny and that's the way to spin it. We're off to the side there, in Manhattanville. We're not in the heart of Harlem—too much historical significance, too hot. It's cooler where we are. With us, on the side there, bringing in new businesses, creating jobs, increasing safety, services—you know the drill, Mike—they are a lot better off with us than if rampant speculators develop willy-nilly. That's the gist of the talking points; you can gussy them up as you see fit. I am happy to feed you guys more by phone, until I am back in my office."

He feels like a used-car salesman, which is puzzling, because he believes in what he is saying. Richard knows he believes in what he is saying.

The COO has asked him to "take a short break." "Family leave," the COO says, over the phone. "Brief, Richard. A week, maybe two, max. A month, tops. Whatever's necessary."

He has no choice but to accept. There will be no reduction in salary. It'll still be his show, Manhattanville. "You can run things from behind the scenes, but don't quote me, Richard," the COO assures him.

The thing is, they don't want to cast any shadows on this venture. It's too important for the university's future. And a "sex scandal" with his kid when he is supposed to be looking out for the neighborhood children is not the image the university wants to project to a nervous community. Already, that bozo Steven Schwartz has started blogging about it. The COO says, "The Schwartz piece, that's the crux of it." Then he quotes Schwartz:

" 'Do you want this man in charge of your kids' school when he can't control his own fifteen-year-old?' That's toxic stuff, Richard. Exactly what we don't need. Plus, the tabloids are having a field day. Thank God, so far you and your family have not yet been named. Still, Page Six! The tuition! The tabloids love the private schools' tuition. But will Bert Anderson? Spelled out in public that way? Anderson's youngest boy is still at St. David's, and his three girls all graduated from Spence. He's not going to want any of that dug up at this late date. He doesn't want to appear like a fat cat, no way."

There's logic in this, Richard sees it. Although a sex scandal seems a ridiculous thing to call it—the girl made the video. He wants to scream this into the phone. Jake just forwarded the fucking thing. It's not his fault. Not really. And it's not bad parenting. Maybe it wasn't the kind of behavior *his* father would have expected from *him*—"You always treat girls honorably," Dad said. "With respect." Hadn't he and Lizzie taught Jake the same thing, albeit in a different language? Hadn't they said, "Safe sex, and better with someone you love"? His son wasn't bad; he was stupid in the moment. So he sent the video to his best friend for help. What does tuition have to do with it? It didn't happen because the kids have money. It happened because they had access to a computer. And how in God's name, in two thousand and fucking three, are you going to stop access to *that*?

But it is ridiculous to fight this battle now, Richard will lose, he sees that he will lose, so it makes no sense to make his case. Better to lie low for a week or two, until Jake is exonerated, or whatever. Until it's out of the papers. But how will he get it offline? There should be a service to suck this kind of stuff out; he'll look into that. Until the school starts behaving like a school. Until the legal questions are resolved—when will that be? Until the girl's family moves away in disgrace, the way teenage girls' families have had to do throughout history. As Lizzie had said the night before half-jokingly, "Don't they know their role?" Richard's got a firm grasp on what it is he needs to do. To save his son. To save himself, he must at least for now give up the job he loves.

"I read you loud and clear, Mike. Thanks for being so upfront. I'll be in touch," he says and then he hangs up.

It's not late enough in the day for a drink, but Richard pours himself one anyway. He keeps a bottle of Laphroaig in his bottom drawer, for late nights, for victory celebrations, for once in a while. He reaches into the drawer and pulls out the bottle and his glass. He pours himself two fingers. It is sort of amazing that it has taken him this long to do what he is finally about to do.

It's not that he is incurious.

Richard goes to the outer office and shuts and locks the department door. He goes back into his office and locks the inner door from the inside. This is not something to be done at home, and he'd avoided doing it before at work, but soon Richard won't have the office to go to, and his assistant is out—lucky her, she's had a long-standing dental appointment. No one will bother him with the door shut anyway. Everyone feels too sorry for him at this point to intrude. These days they're all exceedingly polite and formal, cautiously avoiding him.

Richard takes out his laptop—no way would he download this on his desktop. He'd downloaded the video that very first evening after he'd gotten home, before it was pulled from so many of the sites, before it was listed online and off as child pornography, illegal, a criminal activity simply to click on, but he hasn't had the heart to actually watch the thing. Lizzie watched it. In the head of school's office at Wildwood with Jake by her side—O'Halloran had loved this tidbit, what a lack of judgment on Threadgill's part!—and then again and again on her computer at home at night. She couldn't get over it. She'd told Richard every salacious little detail: the shaved pudenda, the rolls of baby fat—a "muffin top," she'd called it. He'd felt like he'd already seen the performance. But because of some peculiar, sideways sense of honor, Richard just couldn't bring himself to turn it on. Daisy had made the video for Jake; she had not made the video for him.

Although now that Richard has risked and lost so much, it just seems practical to understand what it has all been for.

He sits at his desk. He sips his scotch. He clicks on the file.

It starts.

The bleached hair, the pierced ears, the kilted mini, the schoolgirl-whore. The taunt. "Still think I'm too young?" He knows what to expect; he's been briefed. Of course she's too young. She's an infant, a zygote. The tiny breast buds, the raised skirt, a slash and two yeasty rises. Perhaps she hadn't shaved or waxed, Richard thinks irrationally, perhaps she is just prepubescent. His mind turns to his own daughter. Little Coco: elemental, irrepressible, thoughtless, wild. She was not natively blessed with sound judgment, Coco. She followed her heart. He can see her coming out of the bath, her velvety caramel color, the beauty of her naked body, there's nothing erotic

about it—Coco is a child. But so pretty. When they first brought
Coco home from China, Lizzie said, "Look at her belly, those
tiny toes. Look at the arch of her foot. Her ears. They're like
mother-of-pearl seashells. She's perfect, Richard. *Even her little
vagina.*" She'd said the last part in a whisper, because it was
such a secret pleasure, a parent's pleasure, marveling at the sin-
gular gorgeousness of their child's genitalia.

Richard turns back to the video. To Daisy. What he feels is
close to incredulous. Wasn't she someone's daughter? Hadn't
her parents shared a private joy, when she was born, in the
miracle of her body? The body she has now displayed without
reservation to his ungallant son. And for all the video's dismal
raunch, its tawdriness, for all its sexual immaturity and un-
knowingness, there is something about the way this girl has
revealed herself, the way that she has offered herself, truly
stripped herself bare, that is brave and powerful and potent and
ridiculous and self-immolating and completely nuts. It speaks
to him. Is he crazy? He feels crazier in this moment than he
has ever felt in his life. He feels touched by it. And because the
video is all these things and more, because in some way it is
truly the literal essence of what it means to be naked, because
this Daisy makes herself completely vulnerable and open and
100 percent exposed, it also breaks Richard's heart.

Has he himself ever been that undefended with someone he
loved? With anyone?

The answer is simply no. Richard has never had the courage.
He hasn't known how.

For an instant, Richard feels a loss and a yearning so potent
that he actually quietly cries out. What he hungers for in the

shadow of Daisy's foolish bravery is to break the seal of privacy that surrounds his very core. He wants more than anything else to possess the nerve to make himself known.

He takes another sip of scotch.

Daisy wanted Jake to *know* her. She wanted this desperately, Richard thinks. Was it wrong to crave this kind of union—an erasure of boundaries, a blending of souls—so much so that she was willing to risk all?

Richard does not even genuinely know himself.

This little girl, this *flower*, she was wasting herself, wasting herself on his son. A boy so remarkably dunderheaded that he didn't realize that this gift she made for him, that she gave to him, was too precious and vital to her very survival for him to pass it along like some worthless piece of chain mail.

Who gave Jake the power to seize private property, to expropriate it without the owner's consent? What was wrong with him?

Richard picks up the phone and dials his parents' number. No one answers. He knows no one will answer. No one has answered that number in years. Dad died when Richard was seventeen, too young, too young for Dad, too young for Richard. His mother had passed just before they went to China to bring Coco home—at least Mom had seen Coco's picture, at least she'd met and loved Lizzie, at least she'd had the privilege of watching Jake grow. But right now, all in the world Richard wants is to hear his father's voice. He always had such good advice. His father wasn't educated, and the life they'd lived together, Dad and his mother, all three boys, had been simple and predictable and hard, nothing like the complexity and difficulty Richard faces every day, to be sure, but also without the sophistication and the perks, the travel, the art, the fascinating friends, the powerful circles, the restaurants and vacations and good shoes and artisanal cheese and organic fruit and fine wine, the grace notes that he enjoys at this point as if they were his birthright.

Richard was a golden boy, he is a golden man, but he lacks Dad's wisdom. He knows this to be true. He needs his father's help. There is a part of him that no one, including himself, can access. Could his father help him if he were alive? Is it that missing part of Richard, the thing that Daisy has and he hasn't, that allowed Jake to grow up this blinded? Or was Richard being way too hard on Jake? The way Lizzie said. Were his expectations of Jake and of himself ridiculous? Richard is a grown man with children, but he sure as hell wishes he could talk to his own father. Ask his advice. Where did they go wrong with Jake? What should he do now to help him? How can he rise to this occasion and be the kind of parent that would have made his own father proud? He hangs up the phone. It is no longer a working number. For some odd reason, it has never been reassigned.

The BlackBerry buzzes. O'Halloran.

"I got nowhere with Wildwood's head of legal," the lawyer says, bypassing an introduction. "So we're going to make a preemptive strike. We're going to make the preliminary motions of filing a suit. Wildwood has arbitrarily and capriciously suspended Jacob for an incident that he did not provoke or ask for, that occurred off school property and on the weekend, when school was not in session, and that is a private matter that the school has irresponsibly made public, causing

Jacob irreparable harm. I am going to demand that Wildwood expunge any reference to the scandal from his record and reinstate him in good standing immediately, offering him the proper preceptorial assistance to help make up for the work he's missed, so that he can take his exams on time."

"Okay," says Richard, slowly. "Sounds good."

"And then, if the girl's people file suit, we are going to countersue for slander and entrapment. I've done some research, Richard, and her old man is fucking loaded. He's made a fortune in labels. Calvin Klein. I certainly don't want to slap them with a suit, but I'll tell you what, Jacob could come out of this with a significant college fund."

"Wow, Sean, I don't know," says Richard.

"The boy's been wronged, Richard."

"Yes, but . . ." says Richard.

"You're the boy's father. You'll do whatever it takes to protect your kid. I'm telling you it's better to be proactive than to be stuck on second playing catch-up."

O'Halloran continues: "And if someone close to you wants to leak our side of this to the *Observer* or the *Post*, behind your back, without your permission, you know, viewing the video with the boy and his mother in the room, that sort of stuff—horrendous judgment, embarrassingly shameful—well, worse things can happen. Do you understand what I'm saying?"

Richard understands. A shot across Threadgill's bow.

"You love your kid, Richard," says O'Halloran. "You'll do anything for him."

This is all true.

Richard's father loved him, too. Dad was a family man. He

didn't live so far from the ground. Dad didn't focus on him, he didn't coddle him, he didn't help him with his homework or take his emotional temperature three times a day or do any of the things Richard and Lizzie do now, along with eating and breathing, as a way of life. Dad loved his boys within reason. Dad's was a reasonable, conditional love, the condition being that Richard kept his nose clean, that he always did his best, that he conducted himself with honor.

Richard and Lizzie and the girl's parents, all the other parents at that school—they are both too close to their children and too far away from the ground. They are too accomplished. They have accumulated too much. They expect too much. They demand too much. They even love their kids too much. This love is crippling in its way.

One of his suitemates from Princeton is now the managing editor at a major newsweekly. He'll know exactly where and to whom to leak this story, to an intern or a kid reporter. Someone ruthless and eager and hunting for blood.

It is New York. Everyone instantly goes for the big guns. So Richard goes for the big guns, too.

"Whatever you say, Sean," says Richard. "I'll do it."

And so he does.

They meet the next afternoon at the Princeton Club. It has been a while since Richard was inside the building, and he wonders when things got so bad economically that they opened their doors to house the Columbia Club as well. There is a whiff of tackiness about the arrangement. The Harvard Club is what an Ivy League club should be like, Richard thinks, nursing an old sting—he had chosen Princeton over Yale, but he had not made Harvard. Still, this is where his old roommate suggests they meet for drinks. "It will be quiet," said Paul on the phone. *"Discreet."* Paul has a lunch at 44 at the Royalton, so this stop will be on his way back to the office. They meet at three p.m. A discreet hour if Richard ever saw one.

The barroom has few customers; he'd forgotten how beautiful it is, with its large, rectangular black marble bar, backlit wine case, and Art Deco tile floors. Throughout the room there are both literal and pictorial references to the school and to the crew team. A wooden scull hangs upside down across the ceiling over the bar. Two guys Richard's age in suits and an older woman in flesh-colored panty hose are drinking highballs on high-back chairs. An elderly man snoozes in a leather seat at a table near the windows, as if in an old *New Yorker* cartoon. Richard walks to the end of the dining area and slides onto the room width-long black leather banquet that lines the back wall, behind a small wooden table in the corner. A uniformed barkeep comes over with a bowl of snack mix. Richard orders a scotch on the rocks. He nervously ferrets out the honey nuts from the bowl and pops them in his mouth.

Paul is twenty minutes late, so for twenty minutes Richard inspects the large, handsomely framed color photos of the Princeton canal that hang between the windows. He used to run along that canal when he needed a break from studying. In truth, in the four years he spent at the university, he was most at peace alone on that canal, his arms and legs going, his heart pounding in his chest, his breathing deep and steady. Paul has always had a tendency to be late, even back at school, and now he is a very busy man, so Richard is not surprised that he has to wait. He has a drink and a half cooling his heels. The Laphroaig blunts his edges, and he almost forgets for a while why he is there.

So he is momentarily taken aback when Paul finally enters the room. For a second, seeing Paul, in the afternoon this way, seems like a coincidence, a bit of serendipity, a fluke.

Paul stands in the doorway in a dark double-breasted suit, with a light shimmery tie, a cool blue, almost silvery in color; it exudes a phosphorescent glimmer across the barroom like a neon fish underwater. Paul is tall and lean, handsome. He is the first African American ME of his magazine. A media star. He and Richard have always enjoyed a healthyish rivalry (the "ish" is absent Lizzie's input). Back in college, late at night, in the living room of their suite, they would argue over beers "who had it harder," Paul, the Princeton legacy, with his dark skin and congressman father, or working-class bootstraps Richard.

"You're going to play that son-of-a-postal-worker tune all the way to Carnegie Hall?" Paul liked to taunt, stroking an imaginary violin on his shoulder.

Paul's a smart, arrogant fuck, and Richard hates having to ask him for anything. With the race factor, Richard supposes Paul has traveled further in life against greater odds than he has thus far, and in terms of status, Paul is certainly beating him hands down in the moment.

"Buddy," says Paul to Richard, from the doorway. He signals to the barkeep as he makes his way across the room. "A sparkling water, please, Joe. Lime."

"I'm grateful, Paul," says Richard, standing up, in lieu of a greeting, as Paul approaches.

"Pshaw, man," says Paul, motioning him to sit down again. Paul pulls up a chair. "What I want to know is, is she pretty?"

He'd hit him if he could, but he can't. Richard is asking for a favor. He pops another peanut.

"She's a kid, Paul. He's a kid. They're just kids, the two of them. Remember when we were kids?"

"I remember when *you* were a kid. Is your boy a regular stick-man like his father?"

Richard sips his scotch. Don't dance, he thinks. He wants you to dance.

Richard looks up at Paul. Surprisingly, he feels his eyes get moist. He is a father with a kid in trouble.

"Okay, I get it," says Paul. "What's the lede?"

"She sent it to him, Paul. He was completely unaware, totally blindsided. He didn't ask for it. He didn't want it. He forwarded it to his best friend and the rest is history."

"The lede?" says Paul, as Joe the barkeep comes over with his drink. "Thanks, Joe," Paul says.

"The head of school viewed it in front of Lizzie and the kid. Lizzie says it looked like he was getting off on it. She said his leg was jiggling like he was jerking off."

Here Paul grimaces. "Yeoww. A pretty picture."

"Her old man is worth about a fifty mil; she's rich, spoiled, *deprived*." Lizzie's word pops conveniently into his mind. "They leave her unsupervised for a weekend. She has the entire school over for a party. Kids having sex upstairs, smoking pot, maybe even doing blow. I'm not sure about that, but it wouldn't be hard to find out . . . The parents: word is they launder money in Cyprus. What else? The school won't let him back in, so he's getting a zero on every missed exam. It'll wreck him for college, Paul. And the other students at the school are on his side. They're protesting outside the gates with placards. Is that enough?"

"It's enough," Paul says. "Maybe *we* should think about doing a story."

"Paul," says Richard.

Paul leans back in his chair. "Okay, okay, there's a kid we had interning over the summer who's started stringing for the *Observer*, I'll give her your cell."

"It looked like junior league *Debbie Does Dallas*. I don't know where the girl learned this stuff," says Richard.

"More than enough," Paul says.

That evening Richard goes to the movies. He could have gone home, but he doesn't. He could have helped out at home with the children, but he didn't want to. He wanted to see *Matrix Reloaded*. He loved *The Matrix*. It was a great action picture and he'd loved the homages to Hong Kong action movies and spaghetti westerns. Japanese animation. Western religion and Eastern philosophy. He'd loved how the hero, Neo, broke out of the straitjacket of his life and then discovered the true nature of the world and mastered it. But after handing over his ten dollars and twenty-five cents and going AWOL on his wife ("When did it go up a quarter?" Richard asked the box office manager; "January first," she replied. "Don't you ever go to the movies?"), Richard hated *Matrix Reloaded*. He hated it because it sucked. It took itself way too seriously. It made what was great about the first movie ponderous and boring.

Now, when he enters the apartment, Lizzie is sitting on the couch in one of his old business school T-shirts. He knows from experience that it has been washed and worn so many times the armholes are ripped and the shirt, while shapeless, offers a great glimpse of her breasts. But not tonight. Not post-Paul. Not post-shitty-fucking-movie. She is sitting up on the couch in the dark with her laptop glowing on the coffee table. Her face is lit by the blue-white glow, kind of like she is looking into a fortune-teller's magic ball. She gazes up at him, her still-pretty face a hopeful question mark.

He used to be a slave to that face.

He nods yes.

Lizzie smiles at him. She is grateful to him. This is clear from her smile. She is a mother who is terribly worried about her son. She needs Richard to be who he has become.

He pats her on her shoulder.

Then Richard loosens his tie and walks into the bedroom, alone. He hangs up his jacket in the closet. He sits on the end of the bed. Soon he'll untie his shoes, insert the wooden shoe trees, and put them away in his closet. Soon he'll take off his socks.

．．．

I T WAS BORING STAYING at home. Exquisitely, torturously boring. Like peeling a scab. Painful and oddly absorbing. Jake indulged in his boredom. He examined all the facets of the crystal of his boredom. When he was done with that, he inhaled and memorized its scent. He thought, I never want to forget this specific sensation, and then he wondered why, since he was so miserable. He said to himself, I am a freak! I am a mental patient! And then, after a ridiculous amount of deliberation, he thought, I want to memorize this horribleness so that I never, ever allow myself to feel this way again.

He felt tense all the time, tense and nervous. Scared and embarrassed. Angry and bored. He felt a million ands: and, and, and! Whatever . . . and so bored. So bored out of his skull, so mind-numbingly bored that he couldn't concentrate on anything, could not divert himself out of his boredom—not with music, not with books, not with magazines. His mom wanted him to "read ahead, keep up with his studies," but who was she kidding? Jake couldn't think. He couldn't concentrate. And he certainly couldn't keep up with something if he didn't know what it was he was keeping up with, now, could he? It's not like his teachers were sending him his assignments. It's not like anyone was helping him out. He wasn't allowed on the computer, his dad said. In fact, Dad pretty much *decreed* this—which was fine, it was fucking fine with Jake, although it seemed like his mom lived on hers, while his dad, who'd never once seemed like a hypocrite before, was glued to his CrackBerry. Jake was afraid now to touch the damn thing anyway. The email alone. The hate mail and the "you go, dude" stuff—which was just another form of hate mail, Jake thought; it was hateful and caused him to hate himself—it was all enough to trigger a total meltdown.

The thought of the computer made Jake perspire. It made his underarms and neck and even his ass crack feel uncomfortably moist. The apartment itself felt kind of rank and sweaty—with the three of them locked in there together that way, imprisoned, ensnared, entrapped. Coco kept asking him why he didn't have to go to school—"It's not fair," she said. Nothing is fair, Jake wanted to scream at her. Instead, he just glared when his mom said, "Sometimes schools think it's better for a student to work from home for a while." I'll show you unfair, Jake wanted to shout.

He felt like he was living in a little snow globe, the kind his grandma had always sent him as a kid for Christmas, with some snowscape or Frosty or blah-blah-blah, and when you shook it up shiny flakes of snow would whirl about but nothing could get out.

It was a little like a snow globe at home but a hot one, a humid one, like a Bikram yoga studio snow globe. Jake and his dad had

picked his mom up from a Bikram yoga studio a couple of times
when they lived in Ithaca (his dad would make Jake go in and
fetch her; his dad would get to stay in the car "because I am the
dad," he'd say, ironically and not, which was Dad's way), and the
skin on his mom's neck and shoulders would be sickeningly glis-
tening and the yoga studio itself felt and smelled like the inside
of a sneaker, which was how their apartment felt now, the three
of them there cooking in their own anger and worry and mutual
disappointment. His mom and dad were home all day, fretting,
fighting, blaming him—silently, for the most part, although once
in a while one of them would let a little verbal steam sneak out
through clenched teeth, adding to that horrifically clammy quality. It really blew there in the apartment with him and both of his
parents stuck together now at home.

Hell *is* other people. Whoever said that was right on the
money. If Jake were allowed on the computer he could Google
and find out who it was who'd said it, but he wasn't allowed on
the computer. He wanted to ask Henry who came up with it, but
he wasn't allowed to call him. The lawyer had said, "Cease and
desist with all forms of communication, for the time being. No
texting, no emailing, no IM-ing—do any of you kids talk on the
phone these days, Jacob?" The lawyer had said all this with his
mouth grinning, but his eyes lost in space, focusing on nothing,
which was his way. "No phone calls, big guy," said the lawyer,
"You too, Mom," and Jake watched his mom shiver, probably because the dude wasn't looking at her, either: his eyes might as well
have been made of marble, because they didn't seem to see. But
also because what did Mom *have* if she couldn't run off at the
mouth to someone?

Eyes also tend to beam something out. They emanate light as much as they absorb it. They exude some luminous existent, some weird radiant energy; they take in and they shine out. But not this guy's.

Sometimes Jake thought about Audrey. Sometimes it was kind of nice thinking about Audrey, but usually it hurt. He felt small and like an asshole—he pictured himself like a little yappy, annoying dog, the kind you want to kick—and that's when he'd get really embarrassed and tense and dig his fists into his gut. What must she think of him? Sometimes he made noises, like he cried out a little, or he'd say, "Oh God," or "No, no, no," sort of involuntarily, and his mom would call from the other room, "Baby, are you all right?" which made him feel a thousand times worse and more mortified and ashamed than he'd thought possible. Sometimes thinking about Audrey would lead Jake to thinking about Daisy, and there was nothing worse; there was nothing worse on planet Earth than thinking about Daisy. He pretty much hated her. He pretty much blamed her. He'd been fine before he met her. Why did he go to that party? Why didn't he play video games that night at home like the rest of the world? A lot of times he just plain old felt sorry for her and then he totally hated himself. This is where all this boredom led him: to nasty, painful thoughts.

His dad would at least go for a run. He would take Coco to school in his running shorts and then run home across the park. Some days he'd also run back across the park to fetch her. It was like he was in training for a marathon or something, and Coco was his excuse for working out. Some days Dad didn't even shower in between runs, which had to be adding to the apartment's stink. Every day his dad came home later and later in the morning after dumping the kid at school, so he was either getting slower in his laps around the reservoir—which Jake doubted; his father never got worse at anything, he only improved himself, he only enhanced his time and stuff—or he was running farther. It didn't matter. Who fucking cares? thought Jake; it was just better when his dad was out of the house. Take your time, Dad! he wanted to shout, whenever he went out. When he was home, when Dad was on his BlackBerry or on the phone—he kept calling his old Princeton pal; "Thanks, man," his dad said—or reading the newspaper, or lying on the couch with his eyes closed listening to music on his CD player through his headphones, looking like a bug, when he was actively a passive presence in the house and so forthrightly and obnoxiously not at work, things sucked the most. When it was just Jake and his mom, his mom who kept beaming love and support his way, railing against "that girl," ridiculously on his side, almost unrecognizable, really, in her wicked zest to present him as the injured party and Daisy as the devil, it was almost all right. Jake felt nauseatingly grateful to her for her mom myopia, for her single-note support of him; he also wanted to throttle her, and stick a fork in his own neck whenever she shot him a supportive and loving glance, but that vomit of sick and weak emotion was nothing compared to how bad it felt with Dad: jobless and at home, jobless and at home, jobless and at home, because of him.

It had been a week. Only a week. Only a week to turn his life into something alien, and already, this weird new normal—a normal both so random and predictable that he was already boringly, totally used to it. That's all it was: a week. A little more. Ten days. Because the *New York Observer* came out on Wednesdays. And he'd been sent home from school on a Monday, so it had been

on Day Ten of Jake's exile that the shit hit the fan. Sure, there had
been some early tabloid action, and his mom, glued as she was to
UrbanBaby.com, couldn't stop reading the postings. "Don't these
people have a life?" she'd mumble. "Don't any of them have anything better to do than to make dumb, cruel posts about something they know nothing about? Richard, these mothers are the
Witches of Eastwick. They are venal and jealous and horrible,"
and she'd stay stuck to her laptop like all this online gossip was a
brain adhesive and she couldn't tear her forehead away. "This is
what happens when women don't work," she said. "Please, God,
this should never happen to me." But it was on Day Ten with the
Observer piece ("Prep School Pornathon"; "How cheesy can you
get?" his mom said) that the shit hit the snowblower, big time. It
was so detailed! The *Observer* reporter knew about Jake and his
mom in the headmaster's office, about the three of them watching
the thing together. The Gawker post that followed called this "a
Bermuda Triangle of pedophiliac connoisseurship," and crowed
that "Threadgill isn't the first private school headmaster in NYC
exposed as a lover of 'hard candy'—because last fall, at Uptown
Prep, the principal was caught inviting fourteen- and fifteen-
year-old girls to have sex via online chat rooms." Jake's mom
had blanched at that, reading over his father's shoulder. "This
is so awful, Richard. Threadgill's a creep, sure, but there is no
comparison to that guy hunting down children for sex." His dad
had looked then like he might throw up. He put the paper down
and went out to the park to run again. By the next morning Jake's
story was back on Page Six of the *New York Post*, but it was no
longer a blind item. The Wildwood kids had made T-shirts: "Free
Jake Bergamot." A whole mess of them had staged a sit-in in front

of the school during third period. The *Observer* had started a rallying cry—even though the "Pornathon" piece was obnoxious. It was snarky and obnoxious and made all of them sound like rich, spoiled brats. Which they were; a lot of the kids were rich and spoiled—"spoiled and deprived," his mom said to his godmother, Stacey, on a rare instance when she talked on the phone. But not all of the kids were rich and spoiled. Not Henry and James. Not Jake. He didn't think Audrey was. He'd heard her parents were, like, old hippie social workers who had lived in Northampton or something, until they took her home from China, and then they came to the city, where it was okay to be adopted and Chinese and Jewish, too, and she could go to Chinese school and stuff. She could learn calligraphy and fan dance. Like Coco. Jake had seen Coco fan-dance more times than he cared to remember, he'd seen her make monkey faces when she was supposed to be "composed" before an audience— "Compose yourself, Coco," her dance teacher, Ms. Leung, would calmly call out—he'd seen her take that dumb little fan and, instead of being a butterfly or whatever, poke the other dancers in the butt. Why oh why couldn't he be Coco? She got away with everything.

Jake had heard Audrey lived in an apartment in Riverdale, not a house. Audrey was probably at Wildwood on account of diversity. Hippie diversity. Middle-class diversity. Who was a social worker these days? Someone said her parents were old. With gray hair. That they looked like they were her grandparents. Blue jean skirts and bulky sweaters. Birkenstocks with socks. Jake was used to this look, from Ithaca. But this was only what someone said. He didn't know.

The *Observer* and the *Post* and Gawker and the mothers on UrbanBaby.com made it sound like the whole thing with Daisy had happened because Wildwood's tuition was so high, but anyone anywhere could have made that video, even his dad said this, and anyone anywhere could have hit Forward and Send, and anyone anywhere could have been a total fucking retard like Jake was. It didn't require twenty-five grand a year to get that stupid. All they needed was email, which was pretty much close to free, and a computer, which wasn't but wasn't that hard to get to, was it? Maybe it was? There were computers everywhere Jake went: Internet cafés, libraries, three or four to an apartment . . . Maybe poor kids didn't have access to computers and therefore couldn't fuck up their lives as exquisitely as "Mr. Advantages" Jake could. Maybe when his dad started his public school for poor kids up in Harlem he should make it a computer-free zone. Maybe Jake himself should just join the Peace Corps when he got out of college, as penance. Or Teach for America. Or maybe he shouldn't go to college but should volunteer for the army to show that he wasn't such a spoiled brat, such a "child of privilege." His mom said it was a privilege not to have to join the army as your only hope, and the country was at war, right? Two wars. Except the war in Iraq was almost over. "Mission Accomplished," the headlines read just days before his half birthday. Just a week and a half, really, before Daisy's party. Now it was Jake's name in the paper and it was a little thrilling to see it in the *Post*, in the grainy newsprinty picture stretched across some fat kid's chest. The kid had man-boobs, but the photo had cut off his head. It must have been Zach Bledsoe. It was a little thrilling to see Jake's own name in the tabloids that way, but also kind of excruciating. Dad got off the couch both days to go outside and get the papers, still in his running clothes. So they actually had an artifact to paw.

"They're turning the kid into a folk hero," Dad said to no one when he reentered the apartment, paper in hand. He'd sort of stopped talking to both of them. That is, he still talked indirectly, like a narrator in a play, like Jake and his mom were some unseen audience. But there was no longer a direct address, no light punch to the shoulder, no knuckley noogie on the top of Jake's head, no hug.

You could just read it online, you fucking fossil, Jake wanted to scream at him, as Dad spread the newspapers out on the coffee table, but he didn't.

Jake's mom came up behind him then, when Dad was studying the Page Six item. She put her hands on Jake's shoulders and gave them a rub.

No girl will ever touch me like this now, Jake thought.

"See, your friends are all rallying around you, Jakey," Mom said. "They know you're just an innocent victim."

Right, Mom! he wanted to shout. I am the innocent victim who sent an X-rated video of Daisy Cavanaugh all around the goddamned fucking planet.

But he didn't.

He just said, "Wow." He said it kind of softly. In one week, ten days, he and Daisy had become sort of celebrities. Now they were forever linked and also forever pitted against each other, just like divorcing movie stars.

Billy Bob Thornton and Angelina Jolie.

None of that was boring.

That night, Jake couldn't fall asleep. His dad had passed out on the couch listening to music through his headphones. After she put Coco down—"Just one book, Coco-bear. Mommy has a migraine"—his mom had gone to bed with her laptop, like with a goddamned stuffed animal. The door was open and for hours he could see its glow until it went out.

He didn't know what to do with himself. He shut his door. He tried listening to his iPod. He tried reading comics, magazines, a book. He was almost done with *The Great Gatsby*, which he was supposed to be reading again for school. He'd read it last year for school up in Ithaca. His class this year at Wildwood had probably finished discussing it last week. He'd liked it a lot last year, but less so this year, and then all this bad stuff went down, and there was a character named Daisy and he hadn't continued reading, because it sort of freaked him out. Now he picked the book up from his bedside. He'd dog-eared sections that he'd liked. One quote had reminded him of Audrey, or at least how he'd hoped to feel about Audrey, when he reread it. He looked at the section that he'd highlighted the way they'd taught him. "Always notate," his English teacher back in Ithaca had said. The directive sounded like a rhyme to him, even thought it wasn't. Ms. Katz. She was pretty cool. He'd highlighted last year in pale blue. Under the bright yellow wash of this year's marker he read, "He knew that when he kissed this girl, and forever wed his unutterable visions to her perishable breath, his mind would never romp again like the mind of God. So he waited, listening for a moment longer to the tuning-fork that had been struck upon a star. Then he kissed her. At his lips' touch she blossomed for him like a flower and the incarnation was complete."

In the margin, in light pencil, he'd written "Chinois."

Wow, Jake thought, what an asshole I am. What a total fucking idiot. He flipped ahead toward the end. Who cared that he was now reading out of sequence? He was suspended; he could break the rules at home. He'd read the piece of shit before. His eyes ran down the pages, skimming for info, until they caught on the paragraph he'd sought. "They were careless people, Tom and Daisy—they smashed up things and creatures and then retreated back into their money or their vast carelessness, or whatever it was that kept them together, and let other people clean up the mess they had made."

Jake put the book down. He got up and went to the bathroom. He closed the door and locked it. He opened up the medicine chest. His dad had broken his collarbone a year ago last Christmas. They had been vacationing in California with his dad's family, and Jake's cousin Gary had taken them surfing. Jake had been too scared to try, but not his father. He'd zippered himself up sleek as a seal in his nephew's extra wetsuit. After a couple of wipeouts, he'd gotten up on the board, but one particularly rough wave had sent him soaring and somehow he'd landed hard on the board on his clavicle. The Vicodin the doctor had prescribed in the emergency room were still in the bottle waiting for Dad to pussy up and take one. Now Jake took two. He tiptoed into the kitchen and drank some of his mom's wine and some of the vodka they kept for company—as if they ever had company, as if any of them had a friend left in the world. Jake wanted to fall asleep. He figured if he didn't sleep now he would self-combust.

That night, Jake had crazy dreams. There were so many chapters, so much falling off subway platforms and running in

place on the school steps and climbing the side of his building, that he literally felt older when he woke up, like he'd slept
his way through an obstacle course of years. At one point,
Daisy was running through a field, with a white sheet, like a
superhero's cape, wrapped around her shoulders, and he was
winging clods of dirt at her, hitting and staining the sheet. Although, when Jake looked down at his hands in the dream,
the dirt turned into a sticky, clayey mud, and when he tried to
wipe it off he stupidly wiped it on his pants, and then he pan-
icked and rolled on the ground, getting it on his hair and face.
He woke up a little here and thought, This crap is so obvious,
I am such a loser, I can't even have creative nightmares; and
then he was clawed back into the realm of his dreams. In the
next cycle he was older, way older, but he still lived at home
with his parents and they were really old, they were ancient,
in fact, for part of the reverie they were even dead, and his
mother's skin was falling off her fingers and you could see the
bones. On and on, the endless visions wound; it took all night
and the remainder of his childhood; now he was with Coco,
only she was older than he was and she said, "I'm not your
sister," and Audrey came into the picture and said, "She belongs with me," and he was running after them both, but his
mud-stained jeans were stiff and the girls flew away giggling,
"You stink, you stink." All these nightmare variations sucked,
but Jake couldn't wake up from them, try as he might; all night
long he'd pull out of the weird paralysis of sleep long enough
to say to himself, this is only a dream, this is only a dream, but
of course that's what he'd say to himself when he was awake
these days, so he had no idea, really, what was true and what

was pure hallucination. He'd lost his life when he was awake, and now his nights were worse.

The next morning, Jake got up late. Really late. Vicodin-late. He got up in the afternoon. Around one o'clock. He was surprised his mom had not tried to wake him.

He stumbled a little when he stood up. He shook the sleep out of his head and went into the living room. His mom was sitting on the couch. She was still in her pajama pants. Her hair was still tied up on the top of her head in her sleeping knot. It was after lunch and she hadn't even gotten dressed yet. His dad was sitting at the dining room table. His mom looked like she'd been crying.

"Mom?" Jake said.

She seemed surprised to see him. The corners of her mouth turned up feebly like she was trying to smile. Like she was a stroke victim or something. It made him feel sick inside.

His dad got on the phone then. That is, his BlackBerry started buzzing and he picked it up.

"Yes, Sean," he said, and he began to nod.

"What?" said Jake's mom. Her skin was pale and crinkly. She hadn't done whatever she did to it to make it pink. Jake was in a pair of shorts that he'd slept in. None of them bothered getting dressed anymore, it seemed, except for Coco. But they all still brushed their teeth.

His dad waved his mom away. He kept nodding. His eyes were closed and his eyelashes smashed up against his cheeks. His head was bent. Jake could see a little moon of a bald spot amid all that pepper and salt. His dad nodded to the Crack-Berry like O'Halloran could see him. The guy couldn't have seen him if he'd been standing in the room.

"Richard," his mom said.

His dad held up one finger to shush her. What if it was the fuck finger? Jake thought. That's what he really wants. To flip her the bird.

I am losing my mind, Jake thought.

"Yes, Sean, thanks, Sean, thank God, Sean, yes. I don't know how to thank you," Dad said. He genuflected, he enthused, he gushed.

It was pitiable.

I am losing my mind, Jake thought.

"What?" said his mom. "What?"

His dad turned to his mom. "Sean thinks all the negative publicity has made the board of trustees run scared. That blunder in Threadgill's office . . . The guy might just have to resign, Sean says."

"Threadgill?" said Jake's mom. "The guy is an institution. He's been there thirty years."

"They've cut a deal with the Cavanaughs," his dad said. "And they're willing to let the boys go back to school if they attend out-of-school counseling. He'll be on probation, of course; he's got to keep his nose clean, but he can take his exams . . ."

"Oh, thank God," said his mom. Like someone had discovered the cure for cancer.

She hugged Jake and he could smell the bready smell of her skin. Also, bizarrely, yogurt.

"Thank God," his mom said again.

Even his dad was smiling. Jake could see the overhead light glinting off his teeth.

"Exactly what kind of deal did they cut with the Cavanaughs?" his mom asked.

"Daisy gets homeschooled or whatever the rest of the year."

"It would be child abuse to send her back to that place," said Jake's mom.

His dad shrugged. Maybe yes, maybe no. Dad didn't know. Wow. Dad didn't know something.

"Wildwood helps transfer her into the school of their choice for September. The boys stay on academic probation until they graduate, that's what Sean knows."

"Thank God for him," said Mom.

She sat down on the couch. It was as if all the tension and anger had deflated out of her. She literally looked as if her knees had gone weak. Was this officially "dropsy"? Jake wondered. Or was that when your arms and legs swelled? He couldn't remember. Maybe now he'd be allowed to look it up.

"There's still the possibility of child pornography charges. Sean thinks it unlikely. Who would be the disseminators: Daisy, Jake, the rest of the boys, the eighteen-year-old?"

"Luke," said Jake.

"All?" said Dad. "None? Some? At the end of the day it's almost impossible to note all the postings; there were maybe a million hits on this thing before the websites took them down. I'm not a lawyer, but where do you draw the line?"

"Oh my God," said Jake's mom, her hand rising to her chest, pressing against her heart. "Richard, do you think it's over?"

Jake started to cry then. He wasn't sure why, but he did. Tears slipped down his cheeks.

"It'd fucking better be," his dad said. He walked over to Jake and stood behind him. He leaned over, crossed his arms around Jake's shoulders, and gave him a hug. He kissed the top of Jake's head. He kind of rested his lips there.

"It'll be okay, Jakey," said his dad, speaking into his hair. "It'll be okay, son."

Jake couldn't stop crying then. He cried so hard it was hard to breathe. He cried while his father held him.

Jake ran into Henry and James the next morning on the subway. Ordinarily they all commuted together, but this time the boys did not call ahead, or plan to meet up, and they did not wait for one another at the top of the stairs by the magazine kiosk as per usual—although Jake had been hoping the twins would be standing there magically, as if nothing had changed, when he arrived. He'd been a little late because his mom had wanted to drive him to school and his dad had thought that was a bad idea—sending the wrong impression, like he was guilty or something, or special. They'd argued a little about it at breakfast and then his dad naturally won, because his mom deferred to his dad on stuff like this, because she "burned hot" and his dad was "cool by nature" and kept his head, because his dad "knew from strategy" while she "shot from the gut." Jake's dad was in his running shorts getting ready to take Coco across the park when Jake left. So maybe his dad's "enforced sabbatical" was still on, even while Jake's was off, and Jake was supposed to be "putting this all behind him and getting back to normal."

"That's your job," said his mom. All the quotes were hers. She was the talker in the family.

So Jake put on an Ithaca High School "Little Red" basketball T-shirt and a pair of cargo shorts and grabbed his backpack and took off before she could hug him again and run her fingers across the close-cropped lawn of his hair. He shouted, "Bye," as the front door closed behind him, while his mom was still in the bathroom. He didn't even wait for the elevator because he was afraid she'd come running out of the door into the hall, to kiss him or something. He took the stairs.

In the station, there were some Wildwood kids at the other end of the subway platform whom Jake recognized but didn't personally know, so he kept to himself. He slunk back into the swarm of morning commuters standing in the center of the platform, which was always overcrowded and also too narrow, flanked as it was by local and express tracks on both sides. Jake hated Ninety-sixth Street. There was no wall to press back against while you waited, and it seemed like you could easily enough be knocked into both gutters, like a bowling alley or something, which was kind of a scary thought. It was only after he actually boarded the train and sat down that he saw the twins swing onto the car as the doors were closing, stockier James wedging it open with his body so that Henry could squeeze himself on board. Henry kind of popped into the center of the car, his entrance a little like that guy Kramer on *Seinfeld* reruns. He was a bit wild-eyed as he staggered to a halt. He was all long hair and baggy jeans with his boxers sticking out, and he kind of swayed, in a bent-knee karate stance, gaining his balance. The doors hiccupped open again after that and James walked on. James wore pure Abercrombie, a polo shirt with the moose in the corner, distressed jeans, the whole nine yards.

There were several empty seats, one on either side of Jake and a few across from him. The Dr. Zizmor ads were above the empty seats across the way. Henry loved those signs. "Tighten Skin Without Surgery." "Tighten Skin with Krazy Glue," Henry loved to say, and then he'd goof around by pulling back his cheeks and temples with the sides of his hands so that he looked like he was in a wind tunnel. He loved the yellow and orange and green rainbows behind Dr. Zizmor's bald peanut head. He especially loved to brag about the ads that *used* to be up, before Jake moved to New York. The proctologist ads. "Call 212 MD-TUSCH." Henry loved stuff like that. "You should have been there, dude," Henry loved to say. Because everything was always better, Jake knew, before he'd arrived.

Jake wanted to point out the flyers to Henry but was afraid to say anything. Dr. Zizmor smiled rigidly down at him from above Henry's head. Dr. Zizmor's eyes were too small, like slits. The skin beneath his brows but above his lids hung down over them like theatrical drapes. If he was such an expert, couldn't he tighten that?

"Whoa," said Henry when he saw Jake. "Dude, check out your coiffure."

Jake's hand went up instinctively to feel his buzz cut. He'd forgotten about his hair. Every time he looked in the mirror he didn't recognize himself, for about a million reasons, this being one of them. Also, the fact that the past two weeks had completely altered him, a little like psychic plastic surgery.

That, too.

"Henry," Jake said.

"Dude," said Henry.

The subway took off and Henry surfed the center of the car. James sat down across from Jake and a little to the right. His backpack sprawled out on the seat next to him.

"I'm sorry," Jake said. "I didn't know. I should have realized, but I didn't. I'm an idiot," he said. His voice was kind of shaking when he said it.

He'd been rehearsing this for some time in his room. It was like the minute he saw Henry, he plugged himself in.

"You are an idiot," Henry said.

Henry looked at his brother, then back to Jake. Then back to James.

James said, "You forwarded it. You all did, Hen. For all their trash talk, Luke and McHenry, too. I'm the only guy smart enough to do nothing."

Henry recoiled a little at this; more than anything, he hated to have his intelligence insulted.

"Nothing, but jack off to it," said Henry.

James gave Henry the finger.

"I'm not the pedophile in the family," said James.

"Excuse me, but the taker of *my* virginity was two fucking years older than us."

"She was a real *cougar*, bro," said James, his voice dripping sarcasm. "C'mon, we both know she just didn't want to go to college with her hymen still intact."

No one said anything for a while. Bent-legged, Henry rode the swaying subway car like a skateboard.

Then Jake said it again. "I mean it, Henry. I am totally, completely sorry." For a minute, he thought about getting down on the filthy train floor on his knees. He was a freak! An aberration. His voice sort of shook then. God, he thought, please don't let me cry. Please God, not that, too.

Maybe Henry heard the vocal tremor, because he turned away from Jake, but spoke to him. Like he couldn't bear to look him eye to eye. Henry spoke to Jake while staring at his own reflection in the subway window.

"Dude, I was glad for the three days off."

Oh my God, Jake thought, I love Henry! I have never in my life loved anyone more than I love Henry, and I never will again. Not my wife, not my kids, not anybody. This is the most I can humanly love.

Jake put out his fist, and after a second Henry saw it reflected in the subway window, and turned around and bumped it. Then he swung down onto the seat next to Jake.

"Three days?" said Jake.

"Yeah, I've been back for like a week."

Henry had a week more than Jake outside and in the world. He was so lucky!

"What's it like? School. I mean what's it going to be like to be back?" Jake said. "For me?"

Henry thought for a moment. His eyebrows were like twin caterpillars crawling across his forehead. They met in the middle and rubbed noses.

"For you? Well, pretty much for us, everyone was like we were assholes, but also just boneheads. Some girls spit at us in the hall, you know lesbians and feminists, but most everybody else gets it. Nice girls. Sluts."

"Daisy's world-famous," James said from across the aisle.

"I know that," said Jake.

"Plus, we've all had to go to these assemblies on sex and communication, plus Henry's got shrink sessions—my mom's furious about that," James said.

"She's going to try to get Dad to pay for it," Henry said. "Good luck."

The raw shock of sunshine. The boys blinked like newborn puppies in the daylight as the train exploded out of the tunnel and rose up onto the elevated line. They were almost out of Manhattan now.

"You," said Henry, pointing his finger at Jake, "you're like either a martyr or a murderer, a creep or a sex fiend, a deviant, a sociopath, or just another casualty. To some you're like a hero. Zach Bledsoe says you epitomize the burden of the young American male. He thinks you're the total injured party. 'A supreme exemplification of the double standard,' he says, or maybe it's the reverse double standard?"

He looked to James then.

"Beats me," said James. "I don't claim to understand Zach Bledsoe."

"To some," said Henry, clearly enjoying his own oratory, "maybe you're a fatality or maybe you're a nasty man-whore. I even heard one girl call you 'unchivalrous.'"

"Unchivalrous?" said Jake.

"Yeah, dude," said Henry. "You know, a cad. You're a lout, a yob, a boor."

"True enough," Jake said.

"Who was the girl?" said James, picking his nose. He was bored, but interested.

"Audrey," said Henry.

When Jake got to school it was all a blur of backslapping and glares. One of his teachers, Mr. Carmichael, welcomed him back wholeheartedly when Jake entered the Chem lab.

"The whole thing has been blown out of proportion, if you ask me, Jake," said Mr. Carmichael. "You kids are just kids—kids on steroids. The technology put you all on steroids. But nobody asked me, did they? Nobody ever asks me anything. Not my wife, not you students, nobody in this whole goddamn universe gives a good goddamn about what I think or about what I have to say." Then he handed Jake the ten days' worth of assignments and handouts he'd missed. No one else was that nice. His Deconstructing America co-teacher, Ms. Hemphill (the other one, the pregnant one, was out having her baby), wouldn't address him, even when Jake raised his hand. At lunch, in the cafeteria, Jake was a total superstar. Kids crowded around him. Zach Bledsoe pushed through the crowds to sit next to him.

"What they don't understand is that we live in a postsexualized world," Bledsoe said. "You are the embodiment of the contemporary male, sought after, hunted down, and then, once chewed up and spit out, they say you exploited her. Men of the world unite!" said Bledsoe.

"Shut up," said James.

"Postsexual?" said Henry. "Whatever that is, I don't have it." Everyone laughed. Jake included.

Zach Bledsoe reddened. His man-boobs shook with rage, or maybe it was excitement, Jake wasn't sure. You could see them rattling around inside his Jay-Z T-shirt, like hamsters in a cage.

"You want to know what I think?" said Davis.

Everyone wanted to know. Everyone always wanted to know what Davis thought; he was such a stand-up guy and everyone liked him.

"I think Daisy took control of the situation. I think that's what the parents can't stand. So she was sexy on-screen . . ."

"Sexy? You call that sexy?" Jonas said. "I lost my boner watching that thing."

"You lost it fifty times?" James said.

Jonas smacked him upside the head, but gently.

"You know what I mean," Davis said, looking from one boy to the other. "She did what people used to do in private in a way that got really fucking public."

"With a baseball bat?" said Bledsoe. "People do that?"

"You know what I mean," said Davis. "And what's the shame in that? I mean if everyone suddenly goes public . . ."

"My mom said something like that in the cab on the way back from my lawyer's," Jake said.

"You got a lawyer?" said Jonas. He nodded his head in approval. "That's cool, dude."

Davis said, "That's the future."

"Kids having lawyers?" said Jonas.

"No, being public. Being out in the open. The whole world knowing. So if everyone does it, will anyone care? I mean, a couple of weeks later, do we even care?"

"My mom cares," said Henry. "Colleges care."

"I care," said Jake.

"My dad says Daisy will never get a job now," Jonas said. "And my mom says she'll never get married."

"Look at Monica Lewinsky," said Jonas.

"Look at what?" said James.

"She never got married and it wasn't even this bad," Jonas said. "That's what my mom says. Plus, she got really fat."

No one said anything.

"You know what I mean," said Davis, although they didn't really. They didn't seem to, that is. Jake knew he didn't totally get it himself.

"I mean, if you take away the disgrace factor," said Davis, clearly getting exasperated, "won't all the girls be Daisies?"

"Let's hope so," Jonas said.

Everybody laughed. Jake did, too.

On Friday, Rachel Potter asked Jake out. Rachel Potter was one of the hottest girls in his grade and one of the most popular. She had all this great curly blond hair. She came up behind Jake as he was crossing campus on his way to the gym.

"Hey, Jake," said Rachel, her hair singing in a cloud above her shoulders, like each spiral was a voice in a chorus. She had angel hair, Rachel, and she was wearing a little flouncy blue miniskirt, a filmy white blouse, boots on bare legs. She couldn't have been hipper.

He was surprised she knew his name. Except now everyone did. So he wasn't. He was formerly surprised in the moment, not now.

"Hey, Rachel," said Jake.

She walked alongside him.

"It really sucked what Daisy did to you," she said. She smiled at him as they walked down the brick path across the grass.

"Yeah, well," said Jake. He wasn't sure if Daisy actually did it to him or he to her or Daisy to herself, but he liked Rachel's spin.

"I mean, you didn't ask for it, did you?" Rachel said. She kind of leaned into him when she asked the question, and he noticed that her eyes were very, very blue. Almost as if there were holes in her head and he was seeing the sky behind her. Or mirrors, mirrors at two intersecting forty-five-degree angles reflecting the blue above. Like her eyes were a light box.

"Ask her for what?" said Jake. "The email?"

"To dance for you like that," said Rachel.

"No," said Jake. "I didn't ask for it."

"But did you like it?" said Rachel.

Did he like it? This was never a question anyone had asked him before. He'd been surprised by it, he'd been shocked by it, he'd been excited by it, when he'd first seen it; it felt like icy water, really icy water, with actual shards of ice in it, had been coursing through his veins, so cold and spiky. He'd gotten hard. He'd gotten proud. He'd been appalled, scared; he'd wanted to show off.

"I don't know," said Jake.

"I like to dance," said Rachel. She looked him in the eyes when she said that.

Jake's cheeks flushed hot.

"You're so cute, Jake," said Rachel. "You're blushing."

"I am not," said Jake, but he was. He could feel the rising heat.

"Okay," said Rachel, "you're not," but she was smiling then. Smiling in a teasing way, gentle, not mean, inviting.

"Text me if you want to hang out sometime," she said.

"Okay," said Jake.

And then she said, "I have to go to Latin," and she veered off down another path.

The weekend he spent at home doing homework. Catching up on studying for his exams. His parents wouldn't let him out of the house. There was only one more week before finals. Jake was glad for the work. It kept his mind off everything except the sheer panic of trying to master all the stuff he'd missed, plus whatever he hadn't understood from before. His mom had made his first shrink appointment. It was for Wednesday after school, and his mom, looking up from her computer, had said that maybe he might enjoy it. She'd said she herself had liked going to a shrink, which she did back in the day, before she'd married his father. She said Jake's going might inspire her to go again, too. She said all of this to be encouraging, obviously.

"I don't want him to think of it as punitive," Jake heard her whisper to his father, who didn't seem to care if Jake saw it as punitive or not. His dad was too preoccupied with work. With getting back in. He spent most of the weekend on the phone. On email. He was making his case through back roads or something. Something smart and canny and strategic. Something dadlike.

They parked Coco in front of the TV all weekend. They anesthetized her. His mom even let Coco play video games for hours on her laptop; that is, when his mom wasn't on it herself. No one even made a motion to take Coco to the park. Jake

wouldn't have been surprised if they dosed her juice with Bena-
dryl. They let her skip African dance and ballet; they seemed to
forget about it. It wasn't even clear if anyone ever made her take
a bath. It's almost like it's just us again, Jake thought, and Coco
is a boarder.

On Monday he saw Audrey down the hall, the back of her, that
tiny butt, those tight black jeans, those magical gold slippers. He
started to walk faster to catch up with her, when he saw Luke turn
the corner. Audrey took one look at Luke and turned the other
way. "C'mon, Aud," said Luke. He started going after her. Jake
hadn't seen Luke yet; he was afraid to see Luke, and he didn't
want Luke to see him. "Audrey!" he heard Luke call after her.
So Jake hung back in the hallway, taking a step or two in reverse
when Rachel Potter caught his elbow with her hand.

"You're going the wrong way, Jake," she said. She slid her
hand down his arm and crooked her elbow in the hook of his
elbow. "You've got math now, right?"

"How do you know?" said Jake.

"C'mon, I'll escort you," she said. She started walking him
forward. "I looked up your schedule online."

"Why did you do that?" he said.

"Because I like you," she said. Those clear blue eyes again.
Depthless. That blond curly hair, tied back in a knot at the base
of her neck. She liked him?

As they walked down the hall, Jake saw McHenry coming
toward them.

"Fuck you," McHenry said to Jake. It was the first time the two
boys had seen each other. "You are a total fucking asshole."

Jake stopped in his tracks for a second. He hated McHenry.

McHenry took a step in closer to Jake. His breath smelled bad.
Like tobacco and coffee. He got up in his face. "You should drop
out of school, Jacoby, I'm telling you. We could have gone to jail
because of you. You should fucking drop out."

Jake could feel Rachel's fingers tighten around his arm.

"I should fuck you up," said McHenry.

A crowd was beginning to gather. Jake didn't know whether
to flee or fight. He just stood there dumbly, breathing heavily. He
wondered if he was having a heart attack or a stroke. A seizure.

"Do you assholes want to get expelled?" whispered James. He
sailed right past them. "You'll get everyone in trouble."

"C'mon, Jake," said Rachel. She tugged Jake away, McHenry
hissing after him. "You can run but you can't hide," McHenry said.

All through math class Jake could not listen to a word the
teacher said; his cheeks burned and he could hear his own
blood flowing so loudly through his ears there wasn't room for
words or numbers or sounds. When class let out, he decided
he'd go off campus for lunch. He decided he'd go to the nurse
and call in sick. Anything to get out of there. He let the rest
of the class stream out so he wouldn't have to talk to anyone
as he made his getaway. But Rachel was standing in the hall,
waiting for him.

"C'mon," she said.

They went outside and into the woods.

Wednesday he had his first shrink session. The guy didn't have a
beard, which was a surprise. He was younger than Jake's parents,
Greekish—that is, from here but with a Greek last name. He had

an open collar and a sport coat. His skin was darker than Jake's but still white. He was a good-looking guy, with a strong nose. Silvery sideburns. Although Jake arrived by himself; his mom was waiting for him in the waiting room to pick him up when the forty-five-minute hour was over, like he was a tiny kid or terminally ill or just a prisoner. Like he was a little pet goat.

Friday, after school, Jake finally saw Audrey. That is, he spoke to her.

He'd stayed late in the library so he could avoid people. He was supposedly studying, but his attention consistently wandered off. He kept thinking about dinosaurs. His mind was filled with dinosaurs. Just like when he was little. For some reason he kept thinking about the stegosaurus with a brain the size of a meatball. How could something with so large a body have such a tiny head? How could its plates not have been attached to its bones? In what direction had they truly pointed?

It was impossible to empty his mind enough to study. When Jake tried, it quickly filled with other, more awful stuff. How he felt. What it was like at home. The way his parents now seemed to him like strangers. Dishonor! Ignominy! Lonesomeness! The overriding desire to blame everyone else for his own conduct. The weird thrill he got at odd moments when he felt he was actually getting over. Celebrity! Notoriety! Infamy! Did he even want to go on this way? Being this kind of guy, the kind of guy that did the things he'd done?

He'd rather be a boy. A boy who thought about dinosaurs. It was about six when he looked up at the clock and realized that he'd gotten nothing accomplished. Exam week started Monday. Oh well. Maybe he'd just flunk out.

He decided to grab his books and make his way home. Maybe he'd get off the subway a couple of stops later and get a bagel on Broadway. H&H had the best bagels and they were open twenty-four hours, and often when you bought one, it was still warm. Jake could buy a cinnamon-raisin bagel and a salt. If they *were* warm, he wouldn't even need cream cheese, and he could take a bite first out of one flavor and then alternate it with the other, which is what he liked, the saltiness interchanged with the sweet. He walked out of the library and into the bright, cool evening. The sun probably wouldn't set until somewhere around eight o'clock. He could eat bagels and then go to Riverside Park, jump in the Hudson and drown.

She was sitting outside the library. Audrey. The building was surrounded by mown grass, thick and verdant, like a deep shag pile. All over campus were the flowery accents of scattered pink marble benches. Audrey sat alone on one, her back to him. He had the instinct to run back into the building and so he turned on his heels, but when he faced that freestanding glass library, glowing as if it were set ablaze with books, all that intellectual heat seemed to catapult him back in her direction. In front of Audrey, in the distance, was the cavernous shellacked airplane hangar they called a gym. He would pretend he was walking to basketball practice, if she asked him.

Audrey was smoking a cigarette, even though she was on school property, and she was sitting by herself. On a marble bench donated by some Class-of-Something, or the parents of a kid who died in a traffic accident or in a war. The bench was so pretty, and so was Audrey; she looked like a Chinese character from the back, perched upon it that way, the slim lines of her sleek black hair, her all-black outfit, the black jeans and the tight black T-shirt, all precise little brush strokes. And then there were those gold slippers, the smoky gray veil of her cigarette smoke. The red ember. Like watercolor.

"Hey, Audrey," Jake said.

She turned her head up and to the right to see him.

"S'up, Jake," she said, squinting into the light.

"Do you mind if I sit down?" he said.

"A free country," she said. She turned back to look in the same direction she'd been looking in before he came and disturbed her.

Jake sat down next to her. He dropped his backpack down next to his feet. He stared at the tops of his sneakers. He looked over at her knees, her thighs: even as narrow as they were, they fanned out a little pressed against the marble. Jake wanted more than anything to bury his face in her lap.

Instead he raised his gaze. She was so gorgeous, in a boylike way, her eyes, her nose, her beautiful mouth so totally, elegantly balanced. Her jawline exhibited as a precise right angle, and that inky black hair curved under it. Strong, muscular, graceful, lithe. He realized then, for the first time, that the haircut was asymmetrical. Was that new? Or had it always been that way? It curved longer on the right side. On purpose. Audrey was asymmetrical on purpose. She was perfect but tweaked, which made her even more perfect, Jake thought.

She inhaled again, then tipped her neck back, exposing her long, golden throat, and exhaled up into the sky. So the smoke would not get into his eyes.

"I'm sorry," said Jake.

"Why are you apologizing to me?" she said. "That's kind of funny."

"What do you mean?" he said.

"Well, it's Daisy's life you destroyed, not mine," she said.

"I didn't mean to," he said. "I didn't ask her to do it or to send it to me."

"Who cares?" she said. "We don't ask for a lot of things . . ."

There was silence for a while. His mind reeled; he didn't know how to express himself or how to reach her. He searched for any tool he could use.

"I didn't deal with it very well," said Jake, slowly, he hoped plainly. "I know that it was . . . it was . . . it was unchivalrous of me."

"Unchivalrous?" said Audrey. It was almost as if she hooted a little at the word—*her* word, he thought—except she didn't. "Unchivalrous? An understatement," she said. She took a last drag and dropped the cigarette into the thick, green grass and ground it out with her foot. Then she picked up the butt and put it into the pocket of her black sweatshirt. She was shivering, but it wasn't cold and she didn't put the sweatshirt on. Instead, she crossed her legs in a half-lotus up on the bench.

She looked Jake in the eye. Hers were inky black and she'd lined them with black liner. Lashes, eyeliner, iris—all the same color. The skin on her cheeks shimmered gold, like she'd used that body glitter some girls use, although clearly she hadn't, and her lips were pale and she'd chewed her lipstick off; they were chapped even in May. Her teeth seemed to chatter a little behind them.

"You're cold," said Jake. He picked up her sweatshirt off the ground and offered it to her. It was seventy degrees out.

"Do you have any idea how hard it is to be a girl?" said Audrey, legs crossed, teeth chattering. Ignoring his outstretched hand.

"Yeah," said Jake. "I know. The double standard, you mean?" He brought her sweatshirt into his lap. It was soft. He petted it like a small animal.

Audrey reached down into her bag. It was black suede and had long black fringes with black beads threaded on them. It looked vintage—whatever that meant. Like she'd either spent a lot of money on it or found it in a shop in Brooklyn. She snaked her golden arm into the bag and brought out a pack of Marlboros. She opened it and shook out a cigarette and a lighter. She pressed down on the little pedal of the lighter and lit up. She inhaled deeply, and it was as if her body were a balloon and the smoke lifted her. Like helium, it raised her to her feet. With her standing, her T-shirt rose, and he saw the gold ring piercing her navel. It winked at him for a second, before she exhaled and the T-shirt came back down. Audrey stared off at a stand of trees.

"You are just an idiot boy," she said. "You are all just idiot boys. Someday I'll be old and ugly and nobody will want to fuck me and I won't have to deal with you any longer. I am really looking forward to that," she said.

Then she took back her sweatshirt and tied it around her tiny waist, like the sleeves were a black velvet ribbon and Audrey herself was a package, a precious little gift. She slung that cool bag over her shoulder and she started walking. She started walking away from Jake and all the idiot boys, walking away from the

prison of her youth and beauty and into the hard-fought-for loneliness of her future. Audrey walked away from Jake, down the
path toward the stone gates of the school, and there was nothing
he could do to stop her. Or if there was, he was clueless.

Jake didn't talk about any of that with the shrink on Wednesday.
He'd spent the morning taking his Chem final, and he pretty
much talked about how hard it was and how scared he'd been but
at the end of the day he was feeling pretty confident, "bizarrely
confident" were the words he used with the shrink. He felt like
maybe he'd aced it. His dad had been a whiz at chemistry; his
dad had almost majored in chemistry, and maybe that is why
Jake was so good at it himself. He was like his dad that way;
maybe it was in his genes.

"Do you think you are like your father?" said the shrink. He
was wearing a blue tie that day and no sport coat. The tie was
really blue and shiny and it kind of reminded Jake of Rachel's
eyes, but he didn't talk about that, either.

"No, not much," said Jake.

"Not much how?" said the shrink.

"Well, I'm not much of a runner, and my dad is a great runner,
a long-distance runner. He's also kind of like this genius. He's got
a million degrees and his dad was a post office worker and my dad
was the first in his family to graduate from high school, much less
college . . ." Here Jake's voice ran out.

"And?" said the shrink. "What are you thinking, Jake?"

"That maybe I'll be the first one in my family *not* to graduate
from high school," said Jake. He could feel his own mouth smirk.

Like some offstage puppet master was pulling the corners with strings.

"But you just said you aced the Chemistry final," said the shrink.

"Yeah, but I should have been thrown out of school," said Jake.

"Should have?" said the shrink. "Because of the email?"

Jake nodded, his eyes filling with tears.

"I'm not so sure I agree with you," said the shrink. "And the point is, you weren't thrown out of school, so the school didn't agree with you, either."

"I wasn't thrown out because of my dad," said Jake. "Everything is because of my dad. It's like he's some kind of superhero, and I'm just like this sex offender, *plus* a fucking cripple."

"That's interesting," said the shrink, the skin around his eyes crinkling, indicating amusement. He reached over to his desk and picked up a set of keys, his signal it seemed—grabbing those keys—that their time was up. What was he going to use those keys to unlock? A cage with a gorilla in it? In another one of the offices in the suite? Or was he going to use the keys to lock Jake out? "Whew," the shrink would say, the door safely closed and dead-bolted behind him. "That one's not coming back."

There was a fistful of keys in the shrink's hand; he could use them to rake Jake's face if he felt like it.

"Let's talk about that next week," said the shrink.

And they did. The shrink seemed to like to talk about Jake's father, and Jake wanted the shrink to feel successful. What they didn't talk about was Audrey: Audrey walking away from youth and beauty and sex and boys like him. Audrey eager to be old and ugly and alone. And they didn't talk about Rachel. About how that Friday, after McHenry had cursed him out, when they'd gone together into the woods behind school, Rachel had knelt down in the dirt and leaves and sticks on her bare knees and took his dick in her mouth; about how blue and luminous her eyes were as she looked up at Jake while she sucked him off; or about how he'd taken her head in his hands and moved it, gently at first and then roughly, back and forth around his dick until finally he didn't care at all anymore about Audrey or Rachel or anything else but how *he* felt, and he grabbed her head and he pushed it back and forth as hard as he liked it, so hard it seemed that he might hurt her neck or that Rachel might even choke—she seemed to gag a little—but Jake didn't care, he didn't care and he didn't stop, even when she put up a hand to slow him down or maybe even to push him back; it was like he was jerking himself off in Rachel's mouth and when he looked down, her eyes were half closed; he could no longer see any of that crazy blue, just white, and then his dick slipped out of her mouth and she gasped for air and he came on Rachel's face, shooting across her cheek, some of it landing behind her ear, in her beautiful angel hair.

Jake sort of hated her then, even later, too, when she smiled at him.

· · ·

_____

AS MUCH AS HE hates the public spectacle of standing outside Wildwood at drop-off—"like a stockade in the town square,"
Lizzie said when ceding to him the unhappy task—Richard
stands his ground. He waits, bare-legged, exposed in his running
shorts and his Astor University T-shirt for all to see, until Coco
disappears safely inside the building. She'd wriggled free from
his grasping hand and run pell-mell down the block when she
saw a group of her little friends milling about the red front doors
as they opened, barely tossing her father a goodbye. At least she
is eager to go to school, Richard thinks. He ought to be grateful
for that.

"Hello, Richard," a woman says. She has reddish hair pulled
back in a ponytail and the wrinkly face of a raisin. She wears yoga
pants and a tank top. All the mothers dropping off are in some
kind of workout gear; it is their uniform. Except for the ones who
are obviously going to work. They wear light-colored suits and

pumps, slacks and white blouses and flats. Several have already whipped out their cell phones. One is talking into the air like a madwoman, until Richard spots the telltale earpiece with the long cord like an umbilicus attaching her to her Treo. There are a couple of dads in suits. He is the only male in running shorts. The mom who said hello smiles at him, so he smiles back. It is obviously the right thing to do.

"Good morning," says Richard. He has no clue who she is, but his tone is friendly. Then he leans over to touch his toes. He stands up and lifts his hands over his head and bends backward in a little stretch, as if he is going to execute a rearward-facing dive. He bounces on the balls of his feet, dipping his heels down below the curb one after the other, pedaling them out to stretch his Achilles'. He gives the red-haired mother a little wave and takes off. He always starts slowly at first, springing off of the sidewalk and into the street, warming his muscles with a preliminary jog. He runs next to the stalled traffic—the SUVs, the cabs, the Town Cars with drivers. The sidewalk is too crowded, parents bent over and kissing, parents admonishing, reminding, chasing after kids with a forgotten project, the backpack that they've been toting and are mindlessly about to carry with them to work. Nannies giving big fat bosomy hugs. It is like a scene at a cruise launch, Richard thinks. Ahead, the park beckons with its cool green leaves and fragrant air. He waits until he has crossed Fifth Avenue, threading his way through the cars and buses to the other side, and glances at his watch only when he enters the track. He will do two loops on the dirt. Most mornings these days he does three or four loops. This business with Jake has had only one silver lining: Richard has really improved his time. He returned to work ten days before, but he keeps running. He works from behind the scenes. His deputy is still officially in command, although Richard makes all the decisions. They have meetings today. The thought makes his heart race. He has to get home and shower and change and groom himself. He has to put on a jacket and tie. Two loops and Richard will hit the asphalt and run the sidewalks on the other side all the way back to his apartment. Running will help temper his frustration and anxiety. He wonders if Lizzie has woken up yet. He hopes so, and he hopes not. He hopes so, because if she is awake, if she is awake and doing things, her malaise may have lifted, and he'll have help. But if she is awake, doing things or not, he'll have to deal with her. For the first time ever, Richard is sick of dealing with his wife.

Richard increases his pace. One foot after the other, his arms chugging him forward like pistons, his breath blessedly even, deep, calm. He loves to run. He's always loved to run. These days he's loved it harder, more intensely, even as he's felt more so every day like he is running on a hamster wheel—where is he running to? He's begun to wonder. Still, he loves the release it brings him. Not mindlessness, like Lizzie talks about with yoga— or is it mindfulness?—no, more like a fluidity and ease entering his thoughts. The running, the breathing, takes the weight off his thinking, which is constant these days and transmits across multiple frequencies simultaneously: Should he resign? How can he get back in? Is this the moment to make his move? How has this happened to him? It is a relief, any amount of time when he isn't a prisoner of his own mind.

The last time Lizzie slept in, day after day, waking with a slack face, bleary, features softened into a haze of pain, was before

Coco. Her periods coming month after month, and each time Lizzie, with her intense raised hopes, experiencing this normal bodily function like a miscarriage, a loss. With Jake, it had all been so easy—"Richard, you want to go bareback?" Lizzie had whispered into his ear one night when they were still living in Palo Alto, and even now the memory of it, the memory of the sexiness of it, hit him in the gut. He'd been the one who'd wanted a child right away, which in hindsight seems funny now; she is the one possessed. She wasn't sure, she said; they were so young, she had a career to think of, blah blah blah; later, maybe; they were so happy; didn't they have the right to indulge in that happiness? Lizzie and her equivocating, her dreaming, her torture. But Richard had wanted his own family, he craved the stability, and if they had a child together, he could admit this to himself now, Lizzie would be cemented to him. He'd been afraid of losing her. All the range of feeling, the color, she brought into his life, her moral compass, her clamorous need for him, even her neuroses were at that point still attractive, watching her be alive made him feel alive. He'd envied her her emotional scale. Fixing things for her made him feel strong. And when she was pregnant, when he saw Lizzie naked, belly soaring and round, coming out of the shower, he couldn't help feeling powerful—I put that inside of you, he'd thought, getting high off of it. He couldn't believe his luck. They'd been happy with Jake. Richard moved to the World Bank and then to Cornell, things for him had gone swimmingly, and then, all of a sudden, Lizzie wanted another one. Babies were a little like drugs, he remembered thinking at the time. Jake felt so good, she'd wanted more. Now he wondered, was it just that Jake had been getting older? As Jake grew more independent, was it simply that Lizzie no longer knew what to do with herself?

Richard veers off the path and up onto the reservoir. He doesn't often go this way, his daily run is usually longer, but he suddenly craves the steely blue shine on the water and the openness of the footpath. He looks reflexively at his watch, but he's forgotten his starting time, which is unlike him. Too many thoughts. Too many thoughts. He quickens his pace anyway; he wants to sweat, he wants to breathe hard and long. He'd felt so badly for Lizzie the last time. She was clearly depressed then; she is clearly depressed now, but at this point he doesn't have time for her depression, and he realizes with a start that he does not feel that bad for her. Oddly he feels bad for himself. They are both parents up against it. He is the one who has had to compromise himself. What has Lizzie lost? His compassion has run out.

"We meet again, Richard," a woman calls out to him, sort of flirty. She is race-walking, coming from the other direction. Raisin face. There is no privacy here. They might as well live in a fishbowl. Richard gives her a hearty salute as he flies past.

He has too much to do. He has to settle things with the university, one way or another. Fish or cut bait. He has to get back to productive work. He has to support their family. He has to keep Jake on track. He has to provide Coco with a sense of normalcy. Pay the bills, buy the food, do some of the things that are usually on Lizzie's list, until she snaps out of it. He needs to save them from this miasma. Again.

The COO has not said yes and he has not said no to Richard's coming back as spokesman. The COO has been cooling his heels, "consulting with folks," he said. Consulting with "folks"? Richard wanted to laugh out loud. The COO was born and bred in Boston. The Back Bay. Harvard educated. *Folks*? The story will die down, but is Richard the public face they wanted on the project, when the story could so easily flare up again? "Nothing goes away now, Richard," the COO said. "Forgetting is over."

There are seagulls sitting on the surface of the reservoir. They perch one after the other in a straight diagonal line. There must be a sandbar that they are sitting on, Richard thinks. It is not natural for seagulls to sit in a line like that. How did seagulls get there anyway? They are so far away from the sea. Could there be fish living in the reservoir? Nothing makes sense to him. His shirt is soaked with sweat and is stuck to his skin. He pulls it away with his hand but it slaps back and sticks there.

He exits the track on the West Side. He runs on the surface road uptown, in the jogging lane. He'd given Lizzie shots in the butt every day when they were trying to have another baby. He'd helped her take her temperature, had sex when he was too tired, run home from work because she was ovulating. He'd stood on his head next to her, to make her giggle, when she had to invert. He'd held her night after night when she was crying. He'd done the research, brought the articles home for her about all those baby girls in China. He would have done anything for Lizzie then. He wanted to keep them how they were.

He slows down to a jog. He does what he never does. He slows down. There is no hurry to get home, Richard thinks. I have a meeting later, I have to shower, but there's time. There is time now to walk.

When he leaves the park, he stops at a Chino-Latino place on Amsterdam to get a coffee. Decaf, milk, no sugar. Café Nada, they call it. He drinks it as he walks, and little by little the sweat on his shirt dries off.

So many parties. And bad form, Richard said, not to attend them all.

"We have to make sure that we always behave correctly," he told Liz. "There is no margin for error at this point."

It was just past 9:30. Richard had apparently deposited Coco at school and run his ten miles; undoubtedly he'd also already performed his sit-ups on a mat laid down on the living room rug. He'd showered and finished shaving, when Liz, coffee mug in hand, finally stumbled down the hall to negotiate the strategies of the day. Richard was currently applying lotion to the tender skin where his beard had been. Liz leaned against the doorjamb and sipped; the coffee tasted sour, as if she'd just brushed her teeth, although she hadn't yet. For the new apartment, the COO had promised two full baths, but where did that new apartment exist, on whose list of priorities, now that the university had "concerns"?

Liz yawned. She'd been up late surfing the web and had slept in. She'd missed breakfast with the kids and sending them both off to school. These days, she couldn't seem to shake herself into consciousness; for weeks now, ever since the mess with Jake—or, honestly, could it even have been before that?—she'd felt like she could not force her eyelids open, could not swing her legs over the side of the bed and face the world. This inability to achieve wakefulness seemed somewhat akin to rousing from anesthetics, a subject Liz knew something about: she'd endured five surgical procedures following the secondary infertility that preceded Coco's adoption. Then, like this very morning, she had been an imprisoned sculpture trying to find structure and shape, struggling to escape from a block of marble, captive to her own lethargy. Why get up, she'd thought, before they'd redeployed and gone to China—just to wade into a sea of hopeless hope?

A towel was wrapped around Richard's waist. There were still little droplets of water clinging to the silvering hair on his belly and chest. Once upon a time, and not that long ago, Richard in a towel had been sexy. Kids at school, the apartment to themselves, that sort of thing. But Liz was no longer even sure what "sexy" was, or if it applied to her. "Daisy Up at Bat" had seemingly put an end to all that. Sex as a wild and wooly continent, there to be navigated and explored, had been usurped by her son's contemporaries, just as she supposed she and her cohort had once done to their parents—although perhaps a *tad* less dramatically, Liz thought. Generation after generation of teenagers invading this mysterious and previously "adults only" floating island, laying down the flag of ownership, and declaring the previous inhabitants obsolete. Now it was the kids' turf.

"Thanks for letting me sleep in," Liz said. "I can't remember the last time I did that."

Richard raised his eyebrows but said nothing. He opened the medicine chest and reached for his deodorant.

"Everyone get off okay?" she said. "Jakey?"

Richard nodded.

Liz yawned again. He didn't ask her what she'd been up to all night hunched over her computer, and she didn't volunteer.

She put her mug down on the rim of the sink and did a little forward bend, swaying her hips to get out the kinks. In the past, even such a simple pre-yoga stretch might have been enough to draw Richard in, his arms instantly around her waist, his groin pressing against her butt. But Richard hadn't batted one obscenely lush eyelash in her direction since this whole mess with Jake started. Clearly he didn't need to. He whacked off twice daily, it seemed, running through the park.

Oh, who cared? Who cared, but Liz? There were bigger fish to fry, bigger problems to pinball back and forth between and become exhausted by. Like, the 100 percent new and completely foreign hollowness in Jake's eyes. And Richard's bloody, consuming battles at work. Plus there was their altogether shaky standing in the Wildwood community—now, every afternoon at Coco's pickup, Liz felt like a modern-day Hester Prynne. Increasingly, inescapably, she was filled with a desire to flee.

But most urgent of all, according to Richard, were all these end-of-the-school-year parties to attend—so, so many of them. Mostly Coco's. The child Liz had gone all the way to China to seize and neglect. Coco was so little still. So innocent. So spirited—that was a nice word for it—and sweet. Just thinking about her suddenly made Liz's eyes fill. They had been neglecting her. Liz and Richard had tried their best to shield her these last few weeks—although regrettably that had meant more screen time than anything. It had seemed the easiest way to get her out of the room. This weekend, Liz would take her to a museum. They'd bake cookies. She'd ask Coco what she wanted to do. Liz couldn't flee until she lived up to her responsibilities to her daughter, unless the trajectory of her flight was out the window. And Coco had her end-of-the-year music recital this afternoon, dance class performances (Chinese and African and ballet) this Saturday. There was the class science fair tomorrow. The kindergarten end-of-the-year party on Thursday. Also on Thursday was the kindergarten art show (which seemed somewhat anticlimactic coming after the end-of-the-year party, but this was on account of scheduling, the Lower School email had read). The all-school picnic followed "moving-up ceremonies" Friday a.m.—which, thank God, parents weren't allowed to attend—then one of the class mothers was opening her town house for Sunday brunch. Apparently all the town houses on the block shared a giant, lush, rear garden and paid for a communal gardener, and it was lovely this time of year, said the mom—not bragging but stating—especially with the peonies, which Liz imagined to be in full frontal bloom. The call for Liz's correct behavior thus extended through the weekend, even though her whole life she'd always had about a three-hour time limit on being good.

Liz stood in the bathroom doorway and watched her husband complete his toilette—nails filed, ears Q-Tipped, eyebrows trimmed.

"Do you think you'll be able to make her recital?" Liz asked.

"I'll try," said Richard, "but I have a meeting. It may not be possible. It will be mostly mothers anyway."

"Okay," said Liz.

"Just act normally, like we have nothing to hide," said Richard. "Because we have nothing to hide."

"Aye aye, Capitan." Liz saluted him. She was in yoga pants, a wife-beater. She planned soon to be at the studio, standing on her head. Perhaps with the blood rushing to her brain, she'd see the wisdom of Richard's ways: the value of the public performance, the importance of admiring one's own children before a keenly competitive audience, of being caught beaming behind the video camera, a single hand waving in the air while the other fiddled with a touch pad. A twenty-first-century Buddhist koan: What is the sound of one hand clapping? The karmic root of birth and death leant clarity by the silent applause produced by a proud parent simultaneously tapping on his smartphone.

"If anyone asks how we are, you say, 'We're all okay, thank you for asking.' You end it right there."

"I'm not an idiot, Richard," said Liz. He was pissing her off.

"I'm good at this," said Richard.

Then he went to work. He was still officially on family leave, although he now went into the office every day. According to Richard, he fed Strauss info and then Strauss acted as his mouthpiece. Richard liked him, and usually relished the role of mentor, but this felt more like puppeteering. The COO urged patience, but even Liz wasn't sure if her husband wasn't being played.

Liz's class was at 10:30. It was perfectly timed to give structure and purpose to her morning, so it wouldn't get all flabby and soft around the middle. If she left the house now, she could enjoy a latte and a muffin first. Or she could scramble, do errands and pick up some fish and wine for dinner. She could read the paper, call a friend (except she had no friends, not really; Stacey was still asleep; things between her and Marjorie had decidedly cooled);

she could pay some bills, straighten up the house. She was a stay-at-home mother. She could be nickel-and-dimed to death day after day by boring tasks, but she still had the luxury of time.

Or she could go back to her computer and log on.

After hours spent studying Daisy's video the way she might have analyzed a slide in grad school, Liz had graduated to the wider world of online porn—the professionals. She'd concocted an email confession to Stacey at around two a.m., when she was worrying about herself. " 'Daisy' is a gateway drug!" She never sent it; Liz was now a master at Delete. What she so easily found online via Google both captivated and disgusted her. It was also oddly boring; and yet she found it hard to tear herself away. All she had to do was type in "sex" and she found "passed out, gang fucked and screwed." She found "choking on grandpa's smelly old sperm." She found "teen masturbating," which had nothing on Daisy. Liz couldn't believe Jake had access to this stuff. Free. Legal. Frightening. And the other things, not so free, not so legal, with animals, children; it got so much worse. Of course, Liz had been aware of Internet pornography as a concept, but she'd never bothered to explore it. This is not what people who love each other do together, she wanted to say to Jake—although maybe it was? And what did love have to do with it, except for everything? Wasn't love, or a thirteen-year-old's version of it, what had ignited Daisy? It didn't look like lust.

Liz went into the living room, where, last night, on the sofa with her feet on the coffee table, she'd last curled up, her MacBook warm like a kitten on her lap. The sex Liz had so assiduously prepared Jake for—"safe, with a condom, consensual"—wasn't exactly the sex she'd had as a teenager, and it certainly didn't seem to have much to do with the sex he was confronted with now. Sex in a bed, a parked car, a public park in the dark—sex between two actual people with no spectators, Liz understood. But *this* kind of sex, the kind of sex that had kept her up all night, tireless, violent, addictive, was another beast altogether.

Liz sat down on the couch and slid the laptop onto her thighs. She checked her email. The usual detritus, with a single intimate communiqué from Stacey, who must have woken early to mountain bike up Mt. Tamalpais: "So how's my godson Bob Guccione Jr. holding up? You two cuties are on my mind . . ." A note Liz found funny, insensitive, and hopelessly impossible to answer.

She typed in "feigenbaum/blogspot.com." The past two weeks seemed only to heighten her interest in her old TA. She had to have something to do when she was online and it seemed now that she was online most of the time. Last night's entry had shown up at around four a.m. Recently, Daniel Feigenbaum had found the courage to post some of his novel, several pages a pop. He posted as he wrote, so eager it seemed for confirmation. His current contribution completed the novel's first section, sans prologue: "I am putting my work out there in the hopes of building my readership. I am also interested in any ideas about how I can get published."

Some of the earlier postings had garnered wan, obligatory responses. A coworker named Greta had written, "You are so talented. What are you doing wasting your time writing bullshit ad copy here with us?"

His sister wrote, "I like it, Danny. But isn't this sort of the same book you were working on in grad school?"

Now that the section was complete, there were no responses,

but of course he'd only posted a few hours before, in the middle of the night. The work showed some promise, Liz thought, but sister Feigenbaum was right. It seemed an awful lot like the stuff Liz had read of his twenty-some-odd years before, when he was her TA; it showed shopworn and familiar promise. The circumstances were so recognizable—a coming-of-age story about a talented young writer living in Philly—she actually scanned it for references to the mean story he'd written about her in the graduate literary magazine so long ago, as the streetwise but unrefined, small-titted "Eliza" with the Bronx accent, who "wore her urbanity like a badge." She still remembered that line—still remembered trying to suss out whether or not this was a character deficit or not, and right now she wondered if there was any "urbanity" left in her. Whatever, Feigenbaum's gifts remained. He was smart, funny, but still immature. He hadn't seemed to have developed distance from his own dilemmas or learned how to structure a narrative. At what point did potential, budding and nascent, turn into stagnancy? At what point did stagnancy equal tragedy? Is that what made midlife unendurable for so many? Is that what made each and every day feel so damaging? For one strange and burning moment, Liz wanted to save Daniel Feigenbaum even more than she wanted to save herself. The whole thing would read better, she supposed, if the chapter had some kind of hook.

Liz typed, "My name is Sandra Wilshevsky and I am a literary agent. A friend forwarded your work on to me because it shows flair and facility. Do you have representation? Would you be interested in my notes?" Then she pressed Send.

As soon as she had done so, she couldn't believe herself. She was not manipulative, she didn't think, nor deceitful. Or was she? Pathetically, could it be she felt closer to Daniel Feigenbaum at this particularly dreadful moment than she did to almost anyone else on earth?

Liz looked at her watch. Oh my God, she thought, it's late. Time had wrinkled. She'd missed both yoga and lunch. It was as if she'd fallen into a lunatic fever dream. Soon she needed to begin walking across the park to pick up Coco. Yet there was still so much to accomplish. She had to shower and dress. None of the bills had been paid. She could not be late. She felt a bit panicky. With Coco, Mom's presence was still nonnegotiable.

On the screen, her words turned up magically and inerasably on Daniel Feigenbaum's blog, the clandestine email address she used to log on to all that porn appearing next to the post. Her hands were shaking. What was happening to her?

She knew she shouldn't, but she needed fortification. Post-Feigenbaum and pre-pickup. In order to forget Feigenbaum and to be able to face the gauntlet at the kids' concert, even though she was in a hurry, she got high, blowing the smoke out the bathroom window, just like she'd done as a teenager and, truth be told, during some of the grayer stretches of her marriage, all those long nights when Richard worked late, at the World Bank, at Cornell, especially here in New York, all those long days when work seemed to consume most of his thoughts, when she'd had to be funny or cry or fall apart just to capture his attention—and now every day for the past three weeks. It would make the afternoon somewhat possible.

Before this mess with Jake—after, she'd remained apartment bound—the walk from west to east across the park to transport Coco had been the highlight of Liz's afternoons; her mornings, too. All of it. No matter what the weather, the park was a respite, and this time of year the flowering trees—first cherry, then apple blossoms; now it was the dogwood—made her feel like she'd been starving and was suddenly being fed. She especially loved the skyline that ringed the park across the reservoir; it was as if the buildings themselves were the forest and the park was the town. She still couldn't believe sometimes she actually was a resident of this city. The place was rarefied, striking, closed off, and encapsulated. A village under glass.

Mercifully wasted, Liz showered and dressed as carefully as she could in a sleeveless shift and ballet flats. She Visined and applied her makeup. Hair still wet, she left the apartment, although once over the threshold, she stuck one foot behind her to catch the door with her heel before it shut completely. She hustled back inside and quickly checked the Feigenbaum blog and her email (no response, thank God) and then painfully ripped herself away from the computer's powerful epoxy, an anxious glance at her wristwatch forcing her out of the apartment and into the world.

Richard looks at his watch. He told his wife he would try to make their daughter's recital, but both of them knew that this was highly unlikely. He's stuck in a meeting. Actually, he is stuck outside of a meeting, a meeting with some select members of the board of directors of the Manhattanville Campus Project. Strauss is inside. Richard is in his own office waiting to hear Strauss's report on how the proposals are going over. There is his study on potential architects for the project. There is more research on the school—it is Richard's hope that they will turn it into a School of the Humanities. No one knows how to write anymore, and if you can't write, you can't think. Richard believes this to be true. It will start as a middle school and grow into a high school a grade every year. It will be a school to rival the top-tier schools already in the public school system, but he'll make it available only to neighborhood children, including, of course, the offspring of faculty and members of the administration who will soon be residing in the neighborhood. The school community will then be diverse and guaranteed a middle-class faction. This formula will prove—this was Richard's hypothesis, and he had the studies to back it up—that given proper instruction and small class size and a willing parent population, almost any child can succeed. The meeting has been going on for quite some time, an hour and thirty minutes. For an hour and thirty minutes, Richard has been waiting for his phone to ring. It was a lunch meeting, taking place in a nearby restaurant. Richard has not yet eaten lunch himself. Twice he's gone down to the basement of his building to raid the vending machines, with his office phone placed on Call Forward to his BlackBerry. Twice he's come back upstairs, once with chips and the other, a Kit Kat bar. He is a little nauseated in his hunger. A little dizzy. His desk phone rings. He picks it up. Please let it be Strauss, he thinks, like a kid hoping for a present.

"Richard Bergamot," says Richard.

"Dad," says Jake.

"What's up, Jake?" says Richard. He tries to hide the disappointment in his voice. His mind is on the meeting, on the other call. "Everything all right?"

"I fucked up," says Jake. "Again, Dad." And then he begins to cry.

The crying breaks Richard's heart. The "again" inflames him. "What's going on?"

But all he hears is empty air.

"Get a hold of yourself, Jake," says Richard. Although the empty air frightens him. What now? What more could go wrong with this kid? "Take a deep breath." And then when he still hears no response: "I'm your father. I'm always on your side."

Jake's voice comes out thin and wobbly. "It's the Chem final, Dad. I got a fifty-five."

A fifty-five. A failure. Low enough to blow the terms of his probation. Already. The probation blown already. In just a few weeks' time.

"Shit," says Richard, without thinking.

"I'm sorry, Dad, I really tried. I thought I did better, I really did. When I got the grade back I didn't know what to do. I couldn't call Mom. She'll die, Dad."

The two of them, in cahoots now. Protecting Lizzie. Richard feels another flare of anger. He tries to tamp it down. He is reaching out to you, Richard, he says to himself, in *his* father's voice. Don't let him down.

"Chemistry is Carmichael, right?"

"Yes, sir," says Jake. "Mr. Carmichael."

"He's the one who likes you, right?" says Richard. The one. The only.

"Yeah, Dad, I think so. Yes," says Jake.

"I'll give him a call," says Richard.

"I've been really stressed, Dad," says Jake.

"I'll give him a call," says Richard.

Jake starts to cry again. "I'm a mess, Dad. I'm all screwed up."

"Pull yourself together, Jake," says Richard. "Where are you?"

"School," says Jake.

"Finish up what you need to do there and go home," says Richard.

"Mom's home," says Jake.

"Mom's with Coco," says Richard. "Go home. I'll tell your mother. Just go home when you can."

"Yes, Dad," Jake squeaks out.

"Don't worry," says Richard. "I'll take care of it."

He hangs up the phone. He turns to his computer, Googles the school, and hunts for Carmichael's extension. This should not be done by email, Richard thinks. The poor kid, he has been under so much pressure. Still, they had given him one job, one job, and that was to mind the perimeters of his probation, and he screwed it up. Richard is at war with himself. His son is feckless, a victim, weak, supersensitive. It is as if Lizzie is in the room and he is arguing with her in his head. Still, Jake came to him. That is what they had instructed him to do. "Why didn't you come to me?" Richard had said over and over again after Daisy sent that blasted email. Now Jake has. Richard has to live up to his promise.

He reaches across his desk for the landline to call Carmichael. His plea will be on humanist terms. Jake was a solid chemistry student before this disaster. He's experienced tremendous tension since the whole thing started. Richard will offer to get a doctor's note from Jake's shrink. He and Liz will be grateful if Jake can take a makeup. Richard himself will grill Jake on the material. Richard is forming the conversation into a shape in his head when the phone begins to ring, his fingers hovering airborne above the receiver. Is Carmichael calling him? Are his thoughts so loud that Carmichael can read Richard's mind? Richard picks up the phone.

"Hello," says Richard.

"Richard," says the voice.

"Strauss?" says Richard.

"Scott Levine. How are you?"

A Stanford B-School buddy, now an investment banker. They were on the opposite side of everything in the old days, but they always respected one another. Now Scott is a big muckety-muck at Lehman Brothers. He lives in Greenwich and is already on his second wife. The first one Lizzie always referred to as "Mrs. Scott." They have not met the second, although she and Scott have been married for quite some time. There are kids, Richard thinks, with both women. What is her name again?

"Good, Scott," says Richard. "Great to hear from you."

"I've heard a little about what's been going on over there," says Scott. "Jen still keeps up with all the private school scuttlebutt, and the university's loss might just be my gain, Richard. Any chance you're available after work today for a drink?"

As invitations go, this is clearly a nice one. But truth be told, Richard would say yes to anything from anyone at the moment.

"Where and when?" says Richard.

Liz race-walked her usual route through the park, hurrying down ribbony cement pathways that girded fields of plush green grass, and then along the dusty bridle path and across the Upper Reservoir, which spat her out and down a ramp in the East Nineties. At the base of the incline, she spied something that stopped her. At first she thought it had to be the pot, but then, shuddering with some weird evanescent epiphany, she recognized that it really *was* a raccoon, of all things, scaling the trunk of the tree up ahead of her. The masked, pointy-nosed animal stopped his climb and locked eyes with hers: *We are a pair of outlaws living in an alien land*, he communicated telepathically, before curling up in a cleft between two flowering branches. Nature exists, Liz thought. It triumphs. Even when we seal off the curve of the earth with a concrete carapace or the unfurled carpet of seeded lawns. But there was no time to pause and contemplate the victory of the actual over the fake, or even the simulative. Liz was now trotting down to the gaping open mouth of Engineer's Gate on Fifth Avenue and Ninetieth Street. She was perspiring profusely and could also smell her perfume—still Chanel No. 5 after all these years—plus the blank "cool powder" olfactory mask of her deodorant and her own stinky sweat. Looking south as she crossed against traffic, Liz noted the squat Carvel swirl of the Guggenheim. And even though she was late, and full of dread, practically running, she wasted a few seconds to take it in. Oh God, she thought, I could have loved living here.

She then hurried north up Fifth and turned east, jogging the last half block. Panting a little and out of breath, her heart racing, she gathered in front of the Lower School's stately limestone edifice with the other stay-at-homes, the nannies and the au pairs, a stray father or two—not Richard, a searching glance told her—

because they got props for showing up to events, fathers did, even if they spent the whole time sending and receiving email. At the Winter Concert, from the balcony, the North Dakota of the school's theater, where Liz and Richard had purposefully homesteaded, the darkened auditorium below had looked like the prairie at night—all those BlackBerrys flickering their Morse code like fireflies.

Liz nervously combed her hair with her fingers. It had air-dried and tangled in the breeze. She'd forgotten to pack her brush.

"I hate this shit." Sydney sidled up behind her with her signature feline grace. She was in white today, cropped linen pants suspended off the frame of her hip bones and a skimmy tank dangling from her collarbone as if it were slung loosely on a clothesline. Her skin glowed bronze on her toned arms and shoulders. She was chewing gum. She offered Liz a piece. Liz took it.

"Nobody loves their kids more than me," said Sydney, "but even Clemmie thinks all these events are overkill. She'd rather be at home sucking her thumb and staring out the window."

"She's my kind of kid," Liz said.

Sydney placed a light hand on Liz's shoulder. "How's Jake doing?"

Liz knew she shouldn't—Richard would kill her—but she was stoned and lonely and grateful for the interest.

"Not so well," she said. She twisted her hot hair off her damp neck. And then, as if the truth itself were dawning on her: "Actually I think the word for what he is, is shattered. We've gotten him into therapy, but still . . . I'm honestly ready to shoot myself."

Kevin, the security guard, stepped out in his gray blazer and mushroom-colored slacks, his wide face pink as a rose. "All kindergarten parents and nannies, please join us in the auditorium."

Sydney sent Liz a melty look of sympathy just as the red doors opened. The throngs advanced.

There was a sudden sea change and Liz sailed forward in the crush, like she was in a mosh pit, her feet grazing the ground, carried by the crowd. She swiveled her head to search for Sydney, but Sydney was to the front of Liz now, her short brown bob gleaming sleekly in the sun.

"There you are," said Casey. She had her hair caught back in two pigtails, which somehow made her look older than she was. More pruney, Liz thought. Prunier? She was wearing a Paul Frank top and a tiered crinkly cotton skirt, almost as if she were dressing up as her own daughter for Halloween.

"I have been dying to talk to you," said Casey.

"Oh," said Liz.

"How are you all doing? I saw Richard running this morning."

"We're all okay," said Liz. "Thanks for asking."

Good thing Richard prepped me on that one, Liz thought. She felt a little claustrophobic in the crowd. Maybe that's why she was aware of her heart beating inside her chest. Or maybe it was being high. That sometimes happened. Paranoia. Cold sweats. An anxiety attack. She dug her fingernails into her palms to calm herself.

"My heart goes out to you, Liz, it really does," said Casey.

As they entered the foyer of the school and pressed down the corridor to the theater, Casey grabbed Liz's hand by the wrist. Liz was momentarily grateful for the pressure of her grasp. It grounded her, just when she thought she might astral-project out of her own body and sail off into some form of tempestuous sea.

"Sit with me," Casey said. "I've known the Cavanaughs for years; we're old friends—Peter did Bill's photorefractive keratectomy . . ." She stared hard at Liz. Could she tell that Liz was stoned? Or was Casey just taking note of Liz's confused expression? "His astigmatism."

"Oh," said Liz. She breathed in deep.

They took seats together to the left of the center aisle, mid-auditorium. In the thick of it. Richard would have approved, Liz thought. Now everyone could see that she had nothing to hide, that she held her head high. This was Liz's first real foray out in public, she realized, since the whole sordid affair broke. She couldn't just arrive late, duck her head, grab Coco, and jump into a taxi.

"Sherrie supposedly got pregnant by accident," Casey confided. "Peter has three children from his first marriage. Sherrie was supposed to be the younger, sexy wife—you know, the fun one, the one who's never too tired, that sort of thing. She'd give him blow jobs on the ride up to the country. But then they hit a bumpy stretch after Daisy was born; she gained some weight and I think maybe when Daisy was in the Lower School, Sherrie was hospitalized for depression? Anyhow, Peter let Bill know he had one foot out the door but then she pulled it together and *voilà*.

"She's not very maternal, Sherrie," Casey went on. "I don't think she really wanted a child. Maybe she was just staking her claim on Peter? She's a party girl and likes to collect art."

The lights dimmed, thank God. Liz wasn't sure how to respond to Casey. She didn't know how to feel about all this intense and indiscreet camaraderie. Her face felt red and hot, as if she were embarrassed or blushing or angry or just warm. She wasn't sure. She didn't know if she was supposed to be grateful that Daisy's mother hadn't wanted her and was, thus, conveniently the source of all her daughter's troubles, or if she should feel worse that her own son had played a part in this poor child's endless misery. It occurred to her just then that she had never heard Daisy's mother's name spoken aloud before. Peter Cavanaugh, she'd heard. The father. The family broker. The Wallet. But the neglectful mother, depressed, hospitalized—no wonder Daisy had been overseen by nannies—overweight, inept, formerly fun, no. What a sad and devastating portrait. Not at all how she had imagined the Cavanaughs and their life of splendor. Poor Daisy. Poor Sherrie. Liz knew what depression felt like. Sherrie Cavanaugh must love her daughter, Liz thought. Even if she didn't want her. She must love her to the point of unendurable pain at this very moment. She must also hate herself.

In the dark, Liz's heart went out to Sherrie Cavanaugh. Like Liz, Sherrie Cavanaugh was an art lover who didn't have a job, and was bungling being a mother.

After Liz's father died, when she was a teenager, her mother would often arrive at home in the evenings from her job downtown in a dentist's office too weary to eat; she would undress in the entranceway to their apartment, peeling her stockings down, unraveling as she closed their front door. Mom would then lie down on the couch in her bra and half-slip and chain-smoke the cigarettes that eventually killed her from an agate ashtray that lay like an anchor on her chest. Liz could not forget her mother's hectoring: "You girls have to work hard in school. You've got to have your own careers. Never be dependent on a man for money." Now, with all those fancy advanced degrees behind her—BA, MA, PhD, in the lucrative field of art history no less—"dependent on a man for money" would be the ID in Liz's contributor's notes were she ever to email updates to her various alumni magazines. Trapped and useless, Sherrie Cavanaugh and Liz Bergamot had more in common, perhaps, than their children's mutually assured destruction.

The stage lit up. Jane Perskey, crisp in a light blue pantsuit, walked out of the wings and up to the miked podium. The auditorium rang with polite applause.

"Welcome to the Wildwood Class of 2016 end-of-the-year musicale," she said. "I am sure you will be delighted by what you are about to see and hear this afternoon. But before we begin, I'd like to take the time to ask you to turn off your cell phones and other electronic devices and to let you know that several members of our audience suffer from seizure disorders. In our efforts to cut back on all the flash photography, we will be videotaping the performance and will send you each a copy over the summer to remind you of the splendid year we've had, along with materials on the 2003-to-2004 annual fund."

Jane smiled and winked.

There was diffuse laughter. Like the scattering of leaf piles in the wind.

"We have had a wonderful year with all your wonderful children. Thank you all so much for lending them to us."

Everyone clapped, Liz included. From the wings came the opening strains of Bob Marley's "One Love." One by one, led by Mrs. Livingston, the kindergarteners marched out onto the stage singing, *One love, one heart, let's get together and feel all right.* Coco was number eleven in the lineup and she marched with a shit-eating grin on her face. When she spotted Liz in the audience she started to wave and blow her kisses. "Momma," she shouted. "It's me, Coco B.! It's me!" Liz's heart swelled.

"That's so adorable," said Casey.

"Thanks," said Liz.

Mrs. Livingston gently refocused Coco and helped the children arrange themselves in line. Mrs. Aguado's kindergarten class and Ms. Evans's followed them. Soon the entire stage was three-deep in a multi-culti panoply.

"They look like a Gap ad," Casey said, approvingly.

Indeed they did, except for the fact that they were bedecked in gray pants and skirts and white polos.

The music teacher, Ms. Walton, entered from stage left and took a bow. She raised her baton, and the children all inhaled sharply. She brought it down and they lifted their sweet young voices in song, their throats long, their faces upturned, mouths open like baby birds. Like little gray sparrows.

A cappella, they began to sing:

I'm on my way and I won't look back. I'm on my way and I won't look back, I'm my way, oh yes, I'm on my way.

I asked my mother to take me there. I asked my father to take me there. I asked my teachers to take me there. I'm on my way, oh yes, I'm on my way.

Tears fell unchecked down Liz's cheeks. Casey thoughtfully produced a Kleenex.

"Your mascara's running," she said, helpfully.

After the performance, Liz waited proudly outside with the other parents, who were all now slightly rumpled and clammy-

looking, as if they were just wakened collectively from an afternoon nap. The eager young performers soon cascaded out onto
the street. Most of the mothers were carrying flowers, and Liz
mentally kicked herself for not thinking ahead. She would take
Coco to the nearest Korean grocer and have her pick out her own
bouquet. Then they'd walk over to the gelato shop and she'd buy
Coco whatever she wanted. The topping of her choice, even those
cavity-inducing gummy bears. Liz's buzz had worn off and she
had come down enough to grab a hold of herself. No more tears
for her, just one bright smile for her precious daughter, which she
carefully arranged on her face.

Cries of joy escaped from the crowd. Families clustered happily around Ms. Evans, Mrs. Aguado, and Mrs. Livingston as the
kindergarten teachers shook each child's hand and handed them
over to their respective guardians. No sign of Coco anywhere.

Liz packed in closer. Mrs. Livingston saw her anxious expression.

"Coco B.'s in the restroom," said Mrs. Livingston. She nodded
toward the door. "It's okay. You can go inside." A total breach of
protocol, a parent going in the out exit, but what the hell, Mrs.
Livingston's happy but tired manner seemed to say. It was practically the last day.

Liz entered through the red doors. The air was cooler in the
school foyer than it was out on the sunny sidewalk. She walked
down the corridor and to the left, where the bathrooms were located. She opened the door.

There was Coco, surrounded by a gaggle of giggling girls.
Clementine, Coco S., and two girls Liz didn't recognize. And in
the center of the pack, Coco B. Coco Louise Mei Ping Bergamot.

It took Liz a moment to fully identify what the commotion was all about.

To the delight of her audience, Coco was rolling her narrow hips from side to side while she fluttered her fingers in fanlike motions across her flat chest. Then she pressed her palms against her thighs and suggestively pulled up the hemline of her skirt. Her audience giggled and cooed.

I love to love you, baby, Coco sang in a breathy, high falsetto. *I love to love you, baby . . .*

Clementine sucked her thumb.

"Coco," said Liz, sharply. She could feel the perspiration on her neck and shoulders freeze.

Coco stopped for a moment. "Hi, Momma," she said, with a wide smile.

She turned around, wiggling her buttocks in the air. *I'm feelin' sexy, why don't you say my name, little boy . . .* The girls giggled and screamed.

Still bent over, Coco reached down beneath her pleats to lift her skirt.

"That's enough," Liz said, her voice shaking with anger. She grabbed Coco by the arm.

Coco's eyes went wide. She looked terrified.

Liz tried to make her voice more neutral. Even to her own ears, what came out sounded phony and faux-nice. The way an adult would speak in a cartoon.

"Girls, why don't you all scoot along outside. Your parents must be wondering where you are."

Clementine took her thumb out of her mouth.

"Scoot along," said Liz, shooing the girls through the door.

She still had her fingers tight around Coco's wrist. Coco was squirming.

"Ouch, Momma, you're hurting me," said Coco, loudly. "Keep your hands on your own body."

"Shush, Coco," said Liz. "Be quiet." She put her palms on Coco's shoulders and started steering her out the door. "We're going home."

"No ice cream?" said Coco, turning back to look at her.

"Yes, no. Yes, I don't know," said Liz. "Just go."

She gave Coco a little shove forward.

"You didn't like the concert?" said Coco. She stopped and looked up at her mother. Her eyes were brimming.

"Oh no, yes, of course, it was wonderful, honey, the concert was amazing. You were wonderful, honey," Liz said. "I'm sorry I snapped. I just want to get out of here. Mommy's feeling claustrophobic."

"Could you hear my voice?" Coco said.

"I could hear your voice," Liz said.

She put her arm around Coco's tiny waist, and they started walking toward the side exit.

"Liz!"

At the sound of her name, Liz stopped and turned. Backlit from the sun outside, she could see Sydney's smoky silhouette in the open doorway of the school.

"Have you seen my Clemmie?" Sydney called from down the other end of the vestibule. "Mrs. Livingston said she was in the girls' room."

"Must be the one on the second floor," Liz said, and kept walking.

*   *   *

"What now?" says Richard. He was hoping that the call would be a return from Carmichael or, God willing, the long-lost Strauss, when he heard Lizzie's wavering voice. "What is it and why can't you handle it?"

He doesn't have time for this. He needs Strauss to call him. He needs to prepare himself for the meeting with Scott Levine. He needs to win over Carmichael. Why on earth hasn't Strauss called? It is almost five o'clock. Strauss has been incommunicado all day; whatever it is, can't be good. "Come to think of it, why can't you handle anything, Lizzie?"

"Do you have to be such an asshole?" says Lizzie.

"Do you have to be such a bitch?" says Richard. Without thinking, he swings back at her. He's never spoken to her that way before. Nor she to him.

He hears a sharp intake of breath and then Lizzie hangs up the phone. He stares at the receiver in his hand. Another first. This is the year of firsts.

And since this is the year of firsts, first he contemplates letting her stew. Then his better nature gets a hold of him. He picks up the phone and punches in his home number.

She lets it ring. Once, twice, three times. "Come on," Richard groans out loud. It rings again and then the answering machine picks up.

"Lizzie, honey, pick up the phone," says Richard, knowing that he is being recorded. "Pick it up."

"Hello," she says, coming on the line. He can hear her trying to control her voice.

"I'm sorry," Richard says. "I shouldn't have said that. It's just that I've been waiting all afternoon for a phone call, a call that hasn't come."

Silence.

"I'm under a lot of pressure, Lizzie," Richard says. "And it would help me a lot, a lot, if you took care of things with the kids." He says this with what he intends as patience, but even he hears the frustration bubble out. "I mean, isn't that the deal?"

"The deal? There's a deal?"

"You know what I mean," says Richard.

"I never thought of it in those terms before," says Lizzie, as if musing out loud, "but . . . I do do the lion's share of things for the children, I did move to New York for you, I did back-burner my career to help you build yours . . . Is that what you mean by 'deal'?"

"Come on," says Richard. As if she ever truly had a career. As if she hasn't always been something of a dilettante.

"I have a PhD from Stanford; you have a PhD from Stanford. I turned down that postdoc at Harvard so you could go to the World Bank. Who had better grades? Who won more awards?"

"You turned down that postdoc because you were pregnant," says Richard.

"You were the one who wanted a baby then!" Lizzie says. She is so furious it sounds like she is spitting. "Someone had to take care of him."

Richard feels outside his own body as he speaks. He feels as if someone else is speaking through him. The cold, hard facts funneling out of his mouth.

"The reality is this: the financial responsibility for the family was mine then and it is mine now. I haven't had the luxury you've had to be conflicted. And at this moment, I'm under tremendous pressure to keep the whole thing going. I don't need you calling me for every little hiccup." He takes a breath, confesses: "They won't let me back in, Lizzie. Do you know how that feels?"

"I'm sure it feels awful, Richard," Lizzie says quietly.

He pauses. He wants to tell her what is going on with him. At the same time, he wants to impress her. To comfort her. To let her know it will be all right. Old habits die hard.

"Scott Levine called me, out of the blue. He wants to have a drink. If things don't work out for me here, I think there's a possibility for me over at Lehman. I've heard that they're looking for a chief economist. Maybe it's time to make real money."

"You're going to become an investment banker?" Lizzie says. She sounds incredulous. "I left Ithaca and the life we loved, where the children were safe, where they were happy, we traded all of that in for this horrible, ridiculous mess so you could be a banker? What next, you're going to be a Republican, Richard? You're going to go work in the Bush administration?"

"Do you have to be such a child?" He feels like slapping her.

There is silence on the line.

"Enough of this, Richard," Lizzie says. "Our baby is in trouble. That's why I'm calling you."

"I already put in a call to Jake's teacher. I'm on top of it," says Richard.

"It's Coco. Are you listening? I'm calling you about Coco."

"Not Jake?" says Richard. "This isn't about Chemistry?"

"Chemistry?" asks Lizzie.

The conversation is making no sense.

"He failed Chemistry. The final. He called me from school," says Richard.

"He called you?" says Lizzie, the hurt apparent in her voice.

"I'll work with him, we'll get them to regive the test. If we have to we'll send him to summer school. I already have a call in to his teacher."

"But his probation, Richard."

"I know. I said I have a call in to the teacher. Historically, Carmichael's been fairly sympathetic."

"He must be crushed."

"I put in a call," says Richard. "I'm taking care of it. Now, what's up with Coco?"

"It was after the recital," says Lizzie. "I found Coco with a group of girls in the bathroom." As she goes on, Richard listens.

After Liz hung up, the phone immediately rang again. She let it ring, and then just as the machine picked up, she clicked on the receiver, thinking it was Richard. He'd been so angry; she'd never heard him so angry. There was a horrible new edge to their conversation that had never crawled into their fights before. She was hoping he was calling back, hoping they could find a way to make peace.

"Richard," said Liz, a little breathlessly, into the receiver.

"Oh no, it's Casey," said Casey on the other end.

Liz silently cursed herself for answering. The machine began to scream, that high buzzing sound it emitted in protest whenever it was interrupted. She never picked up. She almost always let the answering machine get her calls.

"Hold on." She crossed the room to the bureau where the answering machine sat and frantically pressed buttons to stop the noise.

"Hello, hello," she said. "Sorry about that."

"I think this is the first time you've ever picked up," said Casey. "I was expecting the machine."

"I thought you were Richard," said Liz, stupidly. She did a little verbal two-step to cover up. "I'm sorry, Casey. I don't mean to be rude, we're just in the middle of something here."

"That's why I'm calling," said Casey. "I'm calling as your friend."

Liz felt her stomach drop.

"I just thought you should know that Sydney and some of the other mothers and I were gabbing after the musicale, and Sydney said you said you were ready to shoot yourself, not unkindly, Liz, but with concern, you know? And she said that you looked stoned and that Jake is under psychiatric observation . . . Anyway, I thought you should know that we're all concerned about you. As your friend, Liz."

Thank God for friends, thought Liz. "Thank you, Casey."

"Anything more I can do to help, just let me know," said Casey.

"I appreciate it," said Liz. "That's enough."

Liz must have sat on that corner of her bed for half an hour after Casey hung up. She was waiting for her hands to stop shaking and for her heartbeat to return to normal.

Then she went into the bathroom and opened the medicine cabinet and found a hair tie. She pulled her hair back into a tight

ponytail. She turned on the water and washed her face, forgetting to first tissue off her makeup. She pulled a hand towel off
of the ring that hung next to the sink and rubbed it across her
cheeks and under the eyes—a rainbow of mascara and eyeliner
and foundation and blush smearing across the terry cloth. She
wet her skin again and lathered up and rinsed, and this time she
used the back of the hand towel to dry off, and it came clean.
She looked at her face in the mirror. Without makeup her skin
was pale and thin. Translucent. You could see right through it
into the tangle inside. The veins in her temples that had always
looked like delicate blue tracings—an architect's sketch—now
bulged slightly against the skin in little gray knots. Liz looked
older than she was used to. It was as if she were peering into her
future face.

She left the bathroom and walked into Coco's room. Coco was
sitting on her bed giving her stuffed animal Buster the Cat a tea
party with real water and saltines and Mint Milanos she'd pilfered
from the kitchen. Already there were several soggy puddles on
her handmade quilt. That was quintessentially Coco. When she
was two, she'd learned to climb out of the crib, and Liz would
find her at 1:30 a.m. at her easel, in a smock, painting with water-
colors. You couldn't hold this one back. The trick was to cultivate
her without breaking her spirit, Liz thought. How exactly does
one do that? Liz sat down on the bed.

"Would you like a cup of tea, Miz Mouse?" Coco asked her.

"Oh yes, Miz Ladybug," said Liz. "Thank you."

Coco splashed some "tea" into a teacup. Up close, what Liz
had taken for water was Paul Newman's Lemonade. There were
sticky patches everywhere. She was about to scold but thought

better of it. The quilt would have to be taken to the dry cleaner anyway. Some of the Milanos had melted.

She took a pretend sip. "Mmm, delicious, Miz Ladybug," Liz said.

Coco was busy arranging what was left of the saltines.

"I loved your concert today, Coco," Liz said.

Coco looked up. "What part did you like best? The way I marched or the way I sang?"

"I loved both," said Liz. "But especially the way you sang."

"You could hear my voice," Coco said.

"I could hear your voice," Liz repeated.

Coco beamed.

"Come sit in my lap," said Liz. Coco crawled over and snuggled up.

"Where did you learn to dance like that, Coco? The way you were dancing for the girls in the bathroom?"

Coco kept her head down, "The movie on Momma's computer."

Liz pet Coco's silky head. Liz had so completely failed her daughter. Is this how Sherrie Cavanaugh felt when she first saw Daisy's email?

"Momma's going to explain to you about that movie," said Liz. "The girl who made it, she made a big mistake. Everything about that movie is a big mistake."

"Why?" said Coco. "Don't ladies dance like that all the time?"

Of course that's what Coco would think. She'd seen it on her own mother's computer. She'd seen stuff like it on TV, probably. The newsstands. In the Halloween costumes at the store, the advertisement for a gym class at the bus stop. It was true, ladies dance like that all the time. And yet Coco was so young, Daisy was so young. Jakey was too young. Everyone involved was too young for this.

"I guess they do," Liz said. "But they shouldn't have to. There is more to ladies than that, more than their—I don't know what to call it—their sexual attractiveness to men, men they don't know."

"I don't understand, Momma," said Coco.

How could she? She was six years old.

"I don't understand, either," Liz said. "And this lady, she's not a lady, she's a girl, she's just a little girl . . ."

Liz's voice broke. Daisy was a just a little girl. She was a baby.

"Then why did she do it?" said Coco.

"Why did she do it? I don't really know. I think maybe she did it to make a boy like her. I think maybe she did it because she felt lonely. I don't know, but I'm sorry that you saw it. I am sorry it was on my computer and I left you alone with it. That was my mistake and I am sorry, truly sorry, Coco."

"It's inappropriate," said Coco.

"Yes," said Liz. "It is. The girl, she didn't respect herself. We women, we always have to respect ourselves . . . Do you know what I'm saying?"

Coco buried her head in Liz's lap.

"Do you know how much I love you?" Liz said.

"Enough to go to China," said Coco. "More than anything."

"Guess who's got the biggest dick in Manhattan?" says Richard.

It is about nine o'clock. He is home late from his drink. Lizzie looks up from her computer screen. He stands in the doorway to the bedroom in his blue suit and tie, which he loosens. Then he stretches his arms out and flashes her his brightest smile.

The bedroom is dark, and Lizzie rubs her eyes as she tears her gaze away from all that backlighting. She quickly closes the laptop lid.

"Where are the kids?" asks Richard.

"In their rooms," says Lizzie.

"I was great today," says Richard.

In the background they can hear the television. "Is that Coco's TV?" Richard asks. Lizzie has let her stay up too late again.

As if she is reading his mind, Lizzie says, "I know it's late, Richard. But it's just cartoons. We had a long talk; I need to tell you about it. After that awful, trying day, I thought, just let her enjoy herself."

"What did Jake say when you got home?" asks Richard.

"'Can we discuss it tomorrow, Mom? Please?'" Lizzie quotes him. "I made him talk a little. He's very upset, Richard. Contrite. I told him we can all discuss it together tomorrow, as a family."

She takes the elastic out of her hair, rerolls it into a little bun as she speaks.

"Then I made them a nice dinner. I tried to normalize things. There's some for you, too, to heat up, if you want it, in the fridge." She snaps the elastic into place and pats her hair down. "I could sit with you."

She looks totally exhausted. But she is trying. Richard sees she is trying.

From the sound of things, sometime in the evening, like worn-out boxers, Lizzie and the kids had each retreated to their various corners of the apartment—Coco to the TV in her room, Jake most likely stretched out on the floor by his bed listening to his iPod, and here in their bedroom, once again, Lizzie heedlessly entering her laptop's dark Oz. Since when do they each need a media highball? Richard thinks. Since when did they need something to take the edge off?

"Turn on the light," Lizzie says.

Richard does, and then he closes the door. And when he does, he sways a little. He reaches a hand out to the wall to steady himself.

"That was one long drink. Are you drunk?" says Lizzie.

"No, I'm not drunk," says Richard. "I am the opposite of drunk." He tries to stand up straight, but he prefers the wall. "Well, maybe a little buzzed, Lizzie. I had a couple of martinis with Scott and then a little celebratory nightcap on the way home."

"Celebratory?" asks Lizzie.

"The job is mine if I want it." He runs his fingers through his hair. He is so proud of himself, he can't stand it. But it does not make sense to show this pride. Let her come to him. Let her come to him in awe. He sways again. He leans up against the wall so that he is looming over her, waiting for her response.

"Sit down, Richard," Lizzie says. "You're not acting like you." There is something close to fear in her voice.

"Really?" says Richard, in surprise. "I think I'm acting *exactly* like me, Lizzie." He laughs. "This is what I do: I save us. We're going to be richer than God."

He grins at her.

"You're acting drunk, Richard," Lizzie says. "Sit down."

She tries to stand up, to put them on more equal footing. But there is no room for her to stand. He is right there in front of her, demanding her approval, her gratitude, her admiration and amazement. He is so close to her, she'd have to push him out of the way to stake her own turf. She is dwarfed there in her chair. He has dwarfed her. She tries to stand, but he is too close, and it looks like her legs won't hold her.

"My legs are half asleep," says Lizzie. "Richard, can't you move back? If you're not going to sit down, I want to stand up. I've been sitting so long they are all pins and needles."

He takes a step back, weaves, regains his balance. It is enough room to allow her to rise. She shakes her legs, one by one. Stamps them a little. She is not giving him her full attention.

"I said, I'm not drunk," Richard says, a bit harshly.

"Okay, okay," she says. "You're not drunk."

"Aren't you going to congratulate me?" Richard asks, so needy he embarrasses himself.

"Of course, honey. Congratulations," says Lizzie, looking up at him. "It's a big job and I am proud they offered it to you."

"Congratulations," says Richard, "but . . ."

"But it's just that money has never been a motivating factor for us before." She takes a step under his arm and finds space on the other side of him.

"Money's never been a motivating factor for you, you mean," says Richard, turning around now to face her. He hears the edge creeping into his voice again. "Because you've never had to worry about it. I do the worrying for you."

Lizzie is quiet. She is thinking. In earnest? Strategically?

Richard is too loaded to be sure. "I appreciate all that you do for us, Richard, I really do," Lizzie says, "but I grew up without a whole lot of money and I can live without a whole lot of money. I just don't want us to lose sight of who we are."

This strikes him as funny. Richard starts to laugh. He puts his forearm on the wall and laughs into it.

"What is it?" says Lizzie. "What's so funny? Richard, honey, please, won't you sit down?"

He laughs and shakes his head.

"Richard," says Lizzie, a little panic creeping into her voice.

"It's just so funny, I come home, once again, saving the day, I come home with the job of a lifetime . . . and you can't even say wow? You can't even say thank you?" Richard is furious. "You say you don't know who we are anymore. Well, join the party. I don't know who you are," he says. His voice is so cold, his body feels so cold. "I don't know who we are anymore, Lizzie."

"We are us, Richard," says Lizzie. "We are us with a child in jeopardy. We are us protecting our child."

"We are not us," says Richard. "Our son does this stupid thing, this terrible thing, and we compound it by being worse."

Lizzie reaches out one hand to touch Richard's arm, but he pulls back. She steps away again, away from him again, and backs up farther into the room.

"He made a mistake, a mistake any grown-up could make," Lizzie says. "You're too hard on him. He forwarded an email. A shocking, grotesque email, an email he didn't ask for. That's all. There was no intentional maliciousness. I'm sure most people would have forwarded that thing on to someone, Richard. Maybe *you* would have."

Richard thinks about the video. He remembers the way Daisy made him feel. He had never in his life felt that way before.

"We never even talk about the girl. We don't even think about her. She is a child," Richard says.

"I think about her, Richard," Lizzie says, facing him off. "Don't tell me what I think about. I think about her a lot."

"You don't think about her the right way," says Richard. "You don't think about her like she was Coco, as if all this had happened to Coco."

"All this *did* happen to Coco," says Lizzie. "How do you think I spent my day? I want to talk to you about it." He can feel the heat of her exhalation on his chest, or is it his heart, on fire? His body is cold but his chest burns.

"That's because you didn't protect her," says Richard, and he points his finger in her face.

Lizzie breathes his accusation in. It's almost as if she accepts and swallows it.

"You're right. I shouldn't have let Coco play on my computer. I should have supervised Coco more closely. I've been so distracted. I haven't paid enough attention to my daughter."

"Our daughter," says Richard.

"Our daughter," says Lizzie.

The phone begins to ring. They both ignore it.

"You're right. I should have protected her . . . It was inexcusable," Lizzie says.

Richard nods in agreement.

"I need help. Help me. I'm . . . I'm . . . I'm flailing. I don't know how to protect them. The genie's out of the bottle. It's in the air. How do I keep them safe?"

Their answering machine picks up. It is Richard's voice. It sounds funny to his ears, jovial, confident, like someone else. "You have reached the Bergamot family. Please leave a message for Richard, Liz, Jake, or Coco . . ."

"You used to play with Jake, when he was her age. You used to do little art projects," says Richard.

A woman's voice comes on the answering machine. "Liz, it's Sydney. I just spoke to Casey and I wanted to let you know I did *not* say you were stoned today at school, I said you *looked* stoned . . . I meant it sympathetically. Call me," says Sydney. "I didn't want to put it in an email."

"You went to Coco's school stoned?" says Richard. He can't believe it.

For a minute, Lizzie looks like she wants to run. But Richard is a wall, standing there in front of her. Forcing her to own up.

"I hate going there, Richard," Lizzie says. "It's all so public. Everyone judging us, judging Jake. You don't know what it takes out of me, every day, just to face it. I should be stronger, but I'm not."

She stands naked before him. It is as if she is entrusting him with her worst secret. People were hard for her, they'd always been. He knew that. These people, they were a totally different animal. Still, he is in no mood to back down.

"Picking up our six-year-old daughter from school? That much you can't handle?" Richard's voice drips with disdain.

Lizzie starts to cry. "I know it sounds pathetic, Richard. I know you're going to roll your eyes. I feel ridiculous even saying it out loud."

Richard waits for her to finish. And when he can't take it another minute—she just stands there sobbing—he practically explodes.

"Just say it, Lizzie."

She wipes her nose with the back of her hand. She uses the pads of her fingers to brush away her tears. "I don't know, I mean, I know it sounds ungrateful, and I am not ungrateful, I am very, very grateful, Richard." She looks him in the eyes. "It's just that this beautiful life . . . I can't manage it," she whispers. "You worked so hard to build it, but I can't manage it. And I don't want it."

"You don't want me, Lizzie?" asks Richard. He feels sweat drip down his back. Is he having a heart attack?

"I want you, Richard. Just not all this," says Lizzie. "I'm sorry. I am really, truly sorry."

He fights the urge to slap her.

"Are you kidding?" Richard says. "What's wrong with 'all this'? You think I wouldn't want to stand on my head all day and lick my psychic wounds? You think during this whole mess I wouldn't have preferred to lock myself in the bathroom and blow a joint?" His voice rises. "But I deal. I deal." He runs his fingers through his hair again. "It's all on me, it's all always been on me. Who are you, Bartleby the Mother? I prefer not to? Grow up, Lizzie."

"Fuck you," Lizzie says. "Go fuck yourself."

"Why did you have me?"

They both turn. Unbeknownst to them, Jake has entered the room, who knew when? Both Lizzie and Richard turn to look at him now. He had heard them fighting, apparently, and is standing just inside the now-open doorway.

"It's obvious you hate me, Dad. It's obvious I ruined your lives." His hands are fists hanging down his sides. His face is red and his eyes are wild.

"That's not true, Jake," says Lizzie. "You made our lives.

You've brought us so much joy. Everything has gotten better since you were born. Everything."

"Cut out the self-pity," says Richard, to Jake. And then to her: "Stop babying him."

"Richard, ease up," says Lizzie sharply. She looks at Jake.

"He's feckless and he's weak," says Richard. "We've made him weak."

"He's had a hard day," says Lizzie. "He's brokenhearted about Chemistry. He thinks he's *failed* you."

"He's failed himself, that's who he's failed."

"That's exactly what I'm talking about," Lizzie says.

She walks over to Jake. She tries to put her hands on his shoulders to comfort him, but he shrugs them off. Tears spill down his face. She stands beside him. She looks at Richard.

"I can take the kids and move them back to Ithaca," Lizzie says.

"No," says Richard.

"I *can* work, Richard, and I can move us away. I'd like to get away from here anyway." She looks at Jake. Jake standing still with his eyes closed, tears streaming.

"I said no," says Richard. "I don't want you to go. I love you." He turns to Jake, but Jake's eyes are shut. "I love them. We are a family," says Richard.

Jake just stands there, trembling, eyes shut, crying. Richard stares at him. He has no idea how to reach him. He has no idea how to be his father. He turns to Lizzie. Now he needs her help.

"I just— Goddamn it, Lizzie, I can do this thing, I know I can," Richard says. "One last time, I can pull it together, be the glue . . . We can have stupid money and we can get our son back on track and into a good school and, with a little luck and a lot of expensive therapy, we can heal our little girl, and you can have all the things you want, but you, the boy, all of you—I've ripped out my guts for you. You've got to see what it costs me."

He sits down on the bed. Richard puts his elbows on his knees and his head in his hands.

"Jake, honey, you should leave the room," Richard hears Lizzie say.

"I want to be a success," says Richard, into his hands.

"You are a success, Richard," says Lizzie.

Richard's shoulders began to quiver.

"I need to be a success," says Richard.

"How much did you drink?" he hears Lizzie say as if she is far away. Down a long tunnel. "Did you eat anything?"

Richard shakes his head, again, without looking up. "Chex Mix. I don't know." His shoulders are shaking, but his voice holds steady.

"Jake, go get your dad two aspirins and a glass of water. If there's a roll left from dinner, bring that, too."

He does not hear Jake move.

"Jake," says Lizzie. "Richard."

"You shouldn't say 'fuck you' to me, Lizzie," Richard says, shaking the head he holds in his hands.

In the middle of the night, Liz got up to pee. Richard was passed out in the bed beside her and snoring lightly—it had been quite late when their fighting and then their talking, their efforts at reconciliation and renewal, had ceased to be productive and, totally spent, they'd joined together only in calling it quits for the night. She'd ended up giving him a Tylenol PM and a glass of water; he needed to sleep if he was going to make it in to work in the morning. Once she'd used the bathroom she returned to their bedroom to get her laptop. She tiptoed down the hall to the living room, sat down on the couch, and opened the computer on her lap. Feigenbaum had written her back that afternoon. She'd read his email after she and the kids had dinner.

"Dear Ms. Wilshevsky," he'd written. "Of course I know you by reputation. And I'd be very eager to send you my work and get your expert response."

Earlier that night, Liz had not known how to reply. She was embarrassed for Feigenbaum and even more so for herself, mortified by her own recklessness. She'd been sitting at her desk thinking about what to do next when Richard had barged in. Richard had looked strange the moment he'd entered the bedroom. She should have realized then that he was in trouble. He'd looked overstuffed. As if someone had put his handsome face on the copier and pressed Enlarge.

Now she reopened her email from Daniel Feigenbaum and clicked on Reply.

"I'm sorry," Liz's fingers tapped against the keyboard, "I really liked what you wrote and I wanted to help, but I don't know how. I'm not who I pretend to be." Then she pressed Send and closed her laptop.

She walked back down the hall to check on her children. First Coco. The little girl was fast asleep, curled up at the foot of the bed, her bottom in the air. There were a few cookie crumbs stuck to her cheek, and as Liz brushed them away she realized they'd never bothered to clean up from the tea party. There was half a cookie stuck to the pillow. Liz picked it up and popped it in her mouth. Probably the sheets and comforter were still sticky. She'd strip the bed in the morning after Coco left for school. She kissed her on her forehead.

Next, Liz tiptoed into Jake's room. He, too, was sound asleep. His ankles hung over the side of the mattress. Jake lay entangled in his sheets, the linens somehow a straitjacket about his waist. She wanted to smooth them out and tuck him in, but she'd only wake him if she tried. He was on his own tonight.

In the years to come, for some reason this moment in recollection took on a totemic importance for Liz. There were many decisions to rethink, obviously, to restring in the whole painful sequence of this debacle, but it was this particular for-instance where she most felt she could have saved them, where she could have saved him, this boy, child of her heart, whom she loved too much. She should have woken him up that night, she thought years later when he flunked out of Princeton as a freshman, or when he drank more than he could handle and their fights grew bloody, especially that one time when she had to confiscate his car keys, throwing them out the window as he lunged; or that horrible rainy afternoon when she dragged him out of the Marines' storefront in Ann Arbor when he threatened to enlist. They had a pretty little house with a garden there during the academic year, she and Coco, near to the ballet school that Coco loved, walking distance to the university where Liz was teaching, and Jake would show up for weeks at a time to sleep in the daybed in the guest bedroom–study, which Richard used for work when he visited on weekends. He'd given her room, Richard, but he never let them go, and Liz was grateful for that. Although it was hard, separated but not. They were on two different tracks now. She'd given him room, too, in her own way, letting him pursue his career on his terms in New York. But when Jake came to visit, she'd experienced none of the wholeness she'd felt when Richard was there lying next to her, or reading to Coco or on the phone in the other room. At night in Ann Arbor, she'd watch Jake sleep then, too, wondering what would become of him, and how to assist him, and about why, on that night now so long ago, she hadn't woken him up, she hadn't sat him up groggily at the end of the bed and said, "I'm sorry honey, I haven't handled this correctly, but there is still time," and told him that it was his job to make some of this right, that she would help him, but he had to own up, own up to what he'd done and to what had been done to him, and once he'd humbled himself before his own faults and misdoings, that he had to learn to forgive himself. Both he and she had to practice the art of self-forgiveness—she should have said this—because although their hearts were good, they were both the type to screw up.

But instead, that night, Liz just stood in her pajamas looking silently down at Jake's cheek, wondering if it was still soft beneath the stubble. He had been the antidote to existential loneliness for her, when he was small. Now she stood by his bedside, on the cusp of finding her wings, helplessly watching him grow.

After grad school, when Richard was working at the World Bank and they were still a young couple, a young couple with a child, they would lie at night in the foldout bed in the living room of their little place in Adams Morgan, above that Senegalese restaurant—what was its name again?—and refer to their home, privately, in whispers, so as not to jinx themselves, as "happy house." The aroma of Yassa au Roulet de la Casamance, the restaurant's signature offering, barbecued chicken in a rich onion-and-lemon sauce, wafted nightly throughout their living room. Jake lay safely ensconced in his crib in the tiny bedroom down the hall. In the summer, that scent was as delicious and as lightly encompassing as the cool sheets that skimmed their bodies. Night after night, she and Richard made love.

Standing at Jake's bedside now, Liz could smell the dish if she concentrated hard enough. When had she last tasted it?

It was so good.

$\bullet$ $\bullet$ $\bullet$

S HE WAS EXITING THROUGH the glass doors of the lobby as
he was entering—he held the door open for her and the heat that
blasted off Broad Street almost was enough to send her back into
the building and up to her desk, where she could order in, but she
forged ahead. He was tall and good-looking in a geeky way, and
he kind of did a double take as she scooted out the door and murmured, "Thanks," and headed down the sidewalk. He looked
like he thought he knew her, but she was in a hurry and couldn't
be bothered. So, even though he was sort of cute, she was a tiny
bit annoyed when he called out her name.

"Daisy?"

She stopped and turned, reluctantly.

Her dad had arranged her summer internship, which came
with a lot of scut work—answering phones and printing out
documents, sorting through crap and walking visitors down the
hall—plus her own email address (dcavanaugh@gs.com—GS,
she told her friends, like "golden sunshine," although everyone

knew it was Goldman Sachs, and that she was lucky), a wardrobe of new shoes, *and* only thirty minutes for lunch, as a result of which she was rushing now, high on top of her stilettos, because there was a new lobster roll place in the neighborhood. One of the summer associates told her it was on Stone Street, and since this was her very first summer not at the beach (she was only flying up on weekends), she craved one.

So she stopped reluctantly when this kid in khakis and a blazer called out after her.

"Daisy," he said it again, and for the first time in a long time she was reminded, out of nowhere, it seemed, that her name was also the name of a flower. Like Hyacinth, or Rose, or Iris.

"Davis," he said. He was sort of preppy, with short hair. "Davis Palmer," he repeated, reminding her. "I was a couple of years ahead of you at Wildwood."

"Yeah, oh, hi," she said. It took her a moment to recognize his name, to place him at all: he was one of the nicer ones. But when she did, her stomach kind of fell.

"So, how's it going?" he said. His eyes searched her face, not unkindly. He looked her up and down, and she wondered for a moment if her skirt was too short. Her hand reached to the hem and tugged it.

"Fine," Daisy said. "But I have only twenty-four and a half more minutes for lunch."

"Are you okay?" Davis asked, staring at her. "I mean, I always wondered . . ."

For a second Daisy worried that she looked faint or red-faced, or that she had ink smeared across her forehead, before she realized what he was referring to.

"You mean 'that'?" she said, raising her eyebrows. Beneath her skin, her cheeks were hot. And that terrible feeling that she used to feel in her stomach all the time, like she was going to throw up or something, returned to her. "It's so long ago, I think of it as kind of humorous."

"Cool," said Davis. And then: "What are you doing down here?"

"I work here," said Daisy. "I mean I work in there." She pointed toward the Goldman Sachs building. "What are *you* doing down here?" She blushed harder. Why did she have to run into him?

"I'm a paralegal," he said, "applying to law school in the fall. I'm meeting a buddy of mine for lunch. A Wildwood guy. Do you remember Zack Bledsoe?"

A fat kid. Now previously fat. Daisy had once thought she'd seen him in the elevator bank; it was kind of hard to tell, because he was half the original's original size—gastric bypass, she remembered thinking as she scooted into the next car to avoid him.

"Speaking of lunch, I've got only nineteen and a half minutes left," Daisy said, looking at her watch. "Bye."

And she ran away from Jake's friend on her high heels toward the Urban Lobster Shack.

She thought she heard him call after her, but she couldn't be sure and she couldn't be bothered.

Daisy was in a hurry and she didn't like to think about all of that anyway. She didn't like to think about those two stupid years she spent away from Wildwood, at that stupid girls' school up in Dobbs Ferry. Things got better when she got back; no one cared that much anymore and Jake was gone, his whole class was gone anyway, and by the time she'd returned, some kids had done much worse: one had jumped in front of a subway and another had taken part in a robbery where a cop died. Plus, there was that scandal with the senator who had twins in the middle school. But as Daisy waited at the takeout window for her lobster roll and chips and slaw and her Honest Tea iced tea, she thought about that first summer after. They had traveled a lot that year, she and her parents. The only constant was that wherever they were, in whichever of their houses, Daisy's windows looked out upon water.

At home, she saw the metallic blue of the Hudson; on the Vineyard, the whitecaps on the icy silver of the Atlantic; in France, it was pure azure all the way, sky and water all the same color; ditto the horizon where they met.

She remembered now her mom had said, "That is how the beach here got its name, Côte d'Azur," which was a big "duh," if you asked Daisy, but nobody asked her.

Instead, she'd spent a long time not reading books, listening to her iPod, flipping through magazines, and not spending time on her computer—she wasn't allowed on her computer then, unless there was an adult in the room, and even her parents got tired of importing and renting adults. Daisy was way too old for a babysitter; everyone knew that and they all got sick of that game pretty quick. Most of the time she'd just lie on her bed or sit in a chair by the window and look out at whatever body of water stretched out endlessly in front of her, and think of him.

Sometimes, in these fantasies, she yelled and screamed at him. Sometimes she kicked him in the balls, or even knifed him in the gut, blood and gore oozing out. The memories of her reveries were beyond embarrassing now. What a little idiot I was,

Daisy thought. She remembered an elaborate fantasy, where she threw shit at him, great big gobs of cow pie or horse manure (she had a horse on Martha's Vineyard and sometimes, after a riding lesson, she thought about mailing some of that horseshit to him in Tupperware, but she worried that they might be able to trace it back to her), and she shuddered now at the thought. Sometimes, with great dignity, she told him off; in her imagination she had these awesome rhetorical skills, while in real life back then (and now), it seemed as if she could barely string two words together. She was trapped and inarticulate; it was even hard to tell herself what she thought, but in her daydreams she made him feel like dirt. She made him feel the same way *she* felt. Other times, she had the regal bearing and grace of a princess, and she sat silently in a tall chair as he kneeled on the ground and begged for her forgiveness.

But whatever the tenor of their encounter, the setting of the denouement was always the same: one of her bedrooms, she in a chair, her hands folded in her lap, Jake on the floor at her feet.

He'd say, "It was my fault, Daisy."

He'd say, "I didn't know. I didn't understand. But now I do."

Sometimes he'd say, "I will spend the rest of my life making this up to you."

Sometimes he'd say, "I wish I could just take it all back. I wish I could make it unhappen. We were just beginning to get to know each other. I could have been your boyfriend. We could have been a couple and gone out."

Always he'd say, "I am sorry, Daisy. I am really, truly sorry."

In all her dreams, Jake apologized. It totally wasn't enough, but it was better than what she'd had.

Then he'd reach out and curl his fingers around hers, and his palm was warm and dry and he'd squeeze tight.

They wouldn't kiss or anything.

He'd just feel bad and hold her hand.

"Lady," said the Urban Lobster Shack guy, waking her up.

Daisy's order was ready, and so she paid up at the takeout counter and took her lunch bag. She looked at her watch.

"Oh my God," she said out loud. It was late, and it was time to get back to work.

She started to trot down Stone Street as fast as she could on those high heels, skittering along on the cobblestones, heading back to the office, her lunch bag flapping against her thigh.

I was a funny kid, she thought, as she ran.

I am still funny.

ACKNOWLEDGMENTS

I am very grateful to Jennifer Barth for her precision and intelligence, to Kristyn Keene for her early and sustaining support, to Elissa Schappell for her sharp eye and Denise Bosco for her gentle lens, and also to Christopher Beha, Morgan Moss, Brian DeLeeuw, Steven Estok, Chin-Sun Lee, Kate Rogan Monahan, and Lila MacLellan. Deepest thanks also go to my patient husband and in-house editor, Bruce Handy, and from the bottom of my heart to Sloan Harris, my most cherished reader.

ABOUT THE AUTHOR

Helen Schulman is the author of the novels *A Day at the Beach*, *P.S.*, *The Revisionist*, and *Out of Time*, and the short story collection *Not a Free Show*. Her fiction and nonfiction have appeared in *Vanity Fair*, *Time*, *Vogue*, *GQ*, the *Paris Review*, and the *New York Times Book Review*. She is an associate professor of writing at The New School in New York City, where she lives with her husband and two children.